The Fibonacci Guestbook

By Sam Hakim

To my mother

"You were within me, but I was outside myself, and there I sought you."
—St. Augustine

ACKNOWLEDGEMENTS

I offer my deepest thanks to my daughter, *Ava*, who sparked the cadence of the chapter titles, especially "The Moment of the Butterfly." Her eyes for small, luminous moments shaped the face and rhythm of this book.

I also thank my friend, *Elaheh*, for the long walks, sharp edits, and timely doubts that made the prose more honest. She showed me where the music faltered and helped me hear it again.

Contents

PROLOGUE

Before the numbers,

before the dreams,

before the house that remembered who you were.

There was silence.

A longing not for answers,

but for something softer:

Recognition.

Return.

To be seen.

We spend years searching outward.

Through cities.

Through lovers.

Through causes, books, and beliefs.

We build names for things we cannot name.

We draw boundaries around the soul

because we fear how vast it truly is.

But sometimes,

rarely,

Something, someone calls you home.

Not to where you began,

but to where you were meant to meet yourself.

A house.

A stranger's voice.

A scent of Sandalwood and cedar in a hallway that

doesn't hold still.

And someone, not new,

but known.

Seen before only in silence.

This is the story

of standing before the question.

Of living within unknowing.

And refusing the comfort of easy answers.

It is the story of a life

lived not in search of replies,

but in the courage

to accompany the questions.

Perhaps there is no answer,

but if we meet the question eye to eye,

hope itself

is already an answer.

This is not the story of this silence or another.

It is the music between the two.

Not the tale of one dream or another,

but the gentle intertwining of both.

This is a quiet revelation,
yet claimed.
A continuous meditation,
yet wordless.
It is the inner voice
speaking to the inner self.

This is not a love story.
Nor a story of death.
Nor even a dream.
This is the moment before the moment,
the breath just before you turn
and finally face the life
that has been waiting for you to enter it.

Sam Hakim
Lisbon, May 2025

1   SOUL AND MEANING

This is a story about two seemingly unrelated
people,
a man and *a woman*.
One searching for meaning.
The other done with meaning and quietly searching
for a soul.
Some stories do not begin where they happen,
but where they are finally heard.
Søren Hussain was a mathematician. A good one.
He taught at a reputable college in Boston.
Where, exactly?
It doesn't matter.
This story isn't about names.
It's about meaning.
Jade Galani was a pilot for a respected European
airline,
Air France or something close enough.
At least, they said it was respected.
Does that matter?
Not really.
Because her story isn't about reputation.
It's about the soul.

Søren taught mathematics.

Does that matter?

Yes.

Because, to him, math had meaning.

Or at least, he believed it was supposed to.

Jade lived in a small but elegant apartment in Paris.

Does that matter?

Yes.

Because Paris had a soul.

And she was still trying to find her place inside it.

Søren had an inner self

but always looked at it from the outside,

like a house glimpsed through its own window.

Jade, too, had an inner self

but she stood inside it, watching quietly,

and found nothing there.

No voice.

No echo.

No one waiting in the rooms.

Jade had her own spirituality,

perhaps quiet, perhaps luminous,

and more than anything:

Free of any overwhelming complexity.

She wasn't seeking to prove anything,

nor was she interested in denial.

She was like an open window facing the light,

just open,

with no need for interpretation.

That spiritual moment among the galaxies,

when she'd dim the unnecessary cabin lights,

switch on the autopilot,

and simply...

Surrender herself to the sky.

It suggested the writings of *Ernest Gann*:

A writer who had lived through nights in flight.

He wrote of that silence,

a silence only found in the cockpit of a night-flying

aircraft,

in the space between the Earth, asleep

and the sky awake.

A place where the darkness outside
slowly seeps into the soul.
At that altitude,
the stars weren't just light.
They were companions,
silent, patient,
close enough to reach between them and touch their
quiet.
Gann once wrote:
"Flying at night
is like hanging between two worlds.
The Earth distant and dim.
The sky was infinite and awake.
And up there,
the pilot doesn't just navigate altitude.
They navigate themselves,
through wonder,
through the interior,
through a presence that is never seen
but always there."
Jade had never said this directly to anyone.
But one night, she set the plane on autopilot,
and let herself, weightless, drift into the galaxies,
and in that moment,

Everything became clear.

The endless sky.

A silent cockpit.

The faint murmur of radio from a distant corner.

And the stars.

Closer than they had ever been.

The night flight from Paris to Nice was quiet.
Smooth. Routine. But something stirred in Jade the
moment she caught sight of him: row 14, seat A.
A small boy, alone. His back straight, big brown
eyes wide. Too still for a child.
There was a tension in his body that didn't belong
to his age, the kind you only acquire by holding
your breath for too many days in a row.
At first, it was just a flicker of recognition, nothing
she could place. But then something deeper.
Something aching.
She had seen this boy before. Not in the terminal.
Not on paper. In her dreams.
The kind of dream that leaves behind a residue, not
in the mind, but in the lungs.

He wasn't *the boy*. And yet, in that stillness, he was.
She gave a short order to the co-pilot and stepped
into the main cabin, ignoring the brief flash of
discomfort in his eyes. She walked down the aisle,
her hands trembling slightly, not from fear, but
from something more disorienting: memory dressed
as coincidence.

"Hi," she said gently. "Do you speak French?"

The boy looked up, startled, then nodded. "Um…
un peu. But I speak English too. My mom says it's
okay."

"Are you flying alone?"

He nodded again. "Yeah. My aunt is going to meet
me in Nice. My mom stayed in Paris."

Then, almost like a confession: "It's my first time
alone."

Jade smiled. "The first time I flew, I was eighteen.
Athens to Paris. I was so stressed."

She remembered gripping the armrest the entire
time, convinced turbulence was a sign from the
universe.

She gestured to the empty seat beside him. "Can I
sit here?"

He nodded. "Okay… yeah. You can."

She sat slowly, folding into the seat like it was heavier than it should've been.

Her body remembered something her mind hadn't yet caught up to.

"You really flew this plane?" he asked.

"I have a co-pilot. Don't worry. I was bored." She smiled. The kind of smile that tries to convince both the speaker and the listener that things are ordinary.

"What's your name?"

"Ali. I'm eight."

"You don't look like the pilots in movies," he said, glancing at her hands. "You're nicer. And… softer."

Jade offered a handshake. "I'm Jade."

He took it. "Hi, Captain Jade."

"What does Ali mean?"

"My mom says it means 'elevated.' Like, high. Or noble." He looked toward the ceiling, then back at her. "I guess that's kind of funny… flying so high."

She didn't laugh. But something warm flickered through her, the poetry of a child who understood metaphor without knowing the word for it.

"Do you ever get scared up there?"

"Oh, thousands of times. See, Ali… fear is primal.
It's okay to be scared. It's normal, as long as you
can deal with it."

He looked down. "Sometimes… I feel like my fear
is too big for my body."

He hesitated. "Have you ever… cried while
flying?"

Jade's breath caught. Her throat burned.

She nodded. "I went to the washroom and sobbed
like a baby."

Ali said nothing at first. Then, like a leaf falling into
the quiet: "That makes me feel okay. Not happy.
Just… like I'm not weird."

Jade turned her hand palm-up between them. A
silent gesture of offering, not of help, but of
solidarity.

Ali didn't take it. But he looked at it. And in that
glance was something older than comfort: trust.

Then he looked up, almost afraid to ask: "Can I see
the stars from your window? In the front? Where
the pilots sit?"

Jade's breath trembled. "It's against protocol," she
whispered. "But since you're an extraordinary,
brave boy, I'll take you."

She paused. "By the way, I saw you listening to music. What was it?"

He smiled. "Just something my mom put on my playlist. No words. You can listen if you want."

Then, more quietly: "It makes the sky feel less empty."

The cockpit was dim, aglow with soft instrumentation. The co-pilot looked up, startled.

Jade gave a single nod. It was enough.

Ali stepped in slowly, like entering a sacred place. When he saw the stars, his mouth opened, but no sound came.

"Whoa," he said finally.

Jade stood beside him, watching his face more than the stars. He didn't ask questions. He didn't need to.

"Do you see that?" she whispered. "That's the Milky Way. Our galaxy."

He nodded. "I think this is the first time I felt big and small at the same time."

And Jade… she broke.

Not visibly. Not loudly. But inside something burst.

She had seen this boy before. But not this way.

He placed one hand on the edge of the console, not touching buttons, just being close.

"Do you think people down there forget this is above them?" he asked.

"Maybe," she said. Her voice barely held.

"Sometimes I think I came from up here," he whispered. "Not heaven. Just… somewhere far and quiet. And I miss it but don't remember it."

Jade's hand twitched, wanting to reach for him. But she held.

"Do you ever feel like you're looking for someone? But you don't know who? Only that you'll know them by how the world sounds when they're close?"

She turned her face away. Tears pooled.

"You are so smart," she whispered. "You're not like an eight-year-old boy."

Ali turned to her. "It's okay. You don't have to answer. Sometimes, I say things, and my mom just hugs me instead."

He looked at her gently. "You don't have to do that either."

"I think you're the one who needed to see the stars tonight. Not me."

Jade nodded, unable to speak.

"Maybe the galaxy is listening," he whispered.

"Maybe it heard both of us before we even said anything."

"Maybe that's why we're here right now. Just for this. Just long enough."

She took him back to his seat.

"Did you get airline toys?" she asked, holding back tears.

"I got a plastic plane. But… it's just plastic."

She smiled. "I have more."

"Can I keep it even if I'm not scared anymore?"

"Yes. Of course."

"Maybe I'll put it next to my bed," he said. "To remember this. And you. And the stars."

She fastened his seatbelt. Her hands trembled.

Then she leaned down.

And finally, she hugged him.

Ali leaned into her, silent tears streaming down her face.

"Thank you, Captain Jade…"

"You didn't just fly the plane. You flew *me*."

Then, almost breathless, almost inaudible: "I think you're the music. The one I was listening to. The whole time."

3 THE WEIGHT WE BEAR

The dream begins with clouds.

Not the kind that drifts in high skies,

but dense, heavy,

as if the sky had collapsed under its own sorrow.

Rain falls relentlessly,

unceasing, endless,

soaking the walls of a nameless coastal village.

Beyond the rocks, the sea slowly rises,

not with rage,

but with intent.

Søren walks among others,

all but one, a broad-shouldered man he's known

before.

In dream, not in waking.

No one else is familiar.

Their movements are quiet,

inward.

They are not actors in this dream,

only witnesses.

And at the center of the square,

that man stands.

His presence is striking,

tall, dignified,

clothed in simplicity.

There's calm in his posture,

and beneath it,

a wornness.

The weariness of someone

who has reached every summit life once promised

and found no air to breathe at all.

The villagers gather around a circular stone

platform.

Their eyes hold fear.

The rain has not stopped in weeks.

The sea is rising.

The flood is inevitable.

No one speaks of it,

but all are prepared.

Small boats are pulled from sheds.

Ropes are fastened.

Oars pass silently from hand to hand.

There is no command,

no leader.

Only a shared understanding:

some must go to the sea.

Not to fight it.

But to face it.

The sea demands a sacrifice,

a mediator between humanity and the sky,

so that its fury may be eased.

Søren watches as the man is the first to step

forward.

Now the boats are ready.

The sea churns with fury and expectation.

The man steps into one of the first boats.

He does not look back.

Others, Søren among them, follow.

Some row. Some drift.

The boats push into depth, into the fog, into the

trembling salt.

Now, the man is standing.

His eyes are open.

His arms rest quietly at his sides.

There is no prayer.

No plea.

The rain softens.

The wind quiets.

A moment stretches,

weightless, suspended.

And then

the man disappears.

No splash.

Not even the sound of a single drop hitting the

water.

His boat simply remains empty.

Silence moves through the dream.

The others gently begin to return.

The sea is no longer a threat.

The village will survive

Though no one will know why.

Søren now lingers at the threshold of sleep and

waking…

On one side stood *Job*.

Not in prophetic majesty,

but in the middle of the earth, wounded in body,

His gaze hollowed out, no longer capable of

meaning.

A quiet curse sat on his lips:

"Why did I not die before I was born?"

Not out of blasphemy,

but from the sheer exhaustion of unanswered
questions.
It was a pain without justification, without
evidence, without meaning.
Job, in Søren's eyes, was the image of a man
defeated
not by the malice of Satan,
but by the goodness of God.
And this was the beginning of burning without
radiance.
No song.
No reward.

And on the other side stood *Prometheus*.
"I stole fire so that humankind might escape its own
darkness.
And my suffering is the price I pay knowingly."
Chained in the *Caucasus Mountains*,
his liver torn open each day,
regenerating by night,
only to be torn again tomorrow.
But he remained silent.
Not out of weakness,
but out of certainty.

His pain had meaning.

His torment had a purpose.

And behind those chains,

there shone a light,

one worth enduring for.

Søren stood between the two.

Torn between two visions,

two gods,

two agonies,

two answers.

In his mind, there was the *God of Jerusalem*,

the one who tested Job,

not with cruelty,

but with silence

as if the aim was not to inflict pain,

but to strip it of all meaning.

And then, there was the *God of Athens*,

born of reason,

who spared no brutality to assert superiority,

but in all that cruelty,

granted Prometheus' pain a purpose.

This paradox would not leave Søren's analytical

mind at rest.

Until that night.

A Twilight Dream:

a man surrendering himself to the storming sea,

in an unannounced sacrifice.

Not for punishment,

but for the salvation of others.

In that moment, Søren understood.

As if a voice had risen from within time,

not from the ocean,

but from *the Cross*:

"My God, my God, why have You forsaken me?"

The hardest test *Christ* faced

was not the nails,

not the crown of thorns,

but the moment he felt distance.

A distance that dragged faith to the brink of denial.

And once again,

the story was about distance.

The distance between *Prometheus'* reason

and *Christ's love*.

In the silence that remained in Søren

after that man's dreamt sacrifice,

he understood:

Sometimes, distance is the answer itself.

He recalled a line he had once read from *Simone
Weil*:
"The moment God hides is not His absence,
but His highest form of presence."
When Søren woke up,
he remembered everything.
The man in the dream,
he was neither a preacher nor an apostle.
But he had witnesses.
And his weariness
was not from sin,
but from all the mountaintops
that no longer made promises.

Søren was, by all accounts, an utterly
unentertaining man.
Each year, the circle of people he could keep
amused grew smaller.
Most people spoke the language of pleasure.
Søren wasn't fluent in that language.
One day, he agreed to a blind date, a meeting
without history or introduction.

He had a peculiar habit: he could only grow

attached to those who, for no clear reason, reminded

him of someone,

someone he couldn't recall.

A face from a dream,

or a presence from beyond memory.

This time, his date was a physician.

And she reminded him of no one.

Søren arrived early.

They had agreed to each bring a copy of a book by

Eckhart Tolle to identify one another.

Søren had taken it as a good sign.

What a delicate, sorrowful thought.

The doctor, not even fully seated, said:

"Oh, you're someone who doesn't know how to

enjoy life, are you?"

The meeting went poorly.

There was no second time.

Although Søren was startled by her shallowness,

he couldn't help but admire her precision.

She was right.

Søren recalled once reading, perhaps via

Wittgenstein, though he wasn't sure,

that while we prepare ourselves for many things,

we do not come into this life to enjoy it.

We drive along the road

and enjoy the scenery,

but the scenery is not the destination.

The doctor didn't connect with these ideas.

Perhaps she didn't understand them at all.

And so, Søren decided not to explain his

philosophy.

She was right in another way, too: Søren had a

fundamental problem with pleasure.

That's why Sara once nicknamed him *the secular*

monk.

Søren didn't quite agree.

To him, suffering wasn't a virtue,

though he sympathized deeply with people like

Simone Weil,

who had chosen virtue through suffering,

but for Søren, suffering was not a virtue.

It was a necessity.

Not because of religious belief,

not mystical revelation,

but because of his worldview:

that pleasure is not authentic,

but suffering is.

And for that reason,

pleasure can never replace suffering.

Søren didn't learn this from psychology.

He learned it from the *Buddha*.

Between pleasure and pain,

there exists a dialectic.

And their synthesis, more often than not, is ennui.

A kind of tired endurance.

Life, he thought, is a pendulum.

Swinging between suffering and boredom.

Between endless wants, essential and trivial, and

the dullness of having.

The error, he said,

is that people see suffering as the opposite of

pleasure.

But they are simply two expressions

of the same unrest.

And liberation lies beyond both.

One day, in a class of half-empty chairs, he spoke

about the mathematics of suffering.

He asked:

If we could add up all the suffering in the world,

war, illness, heartbreak, exile, poverty,

quantify them, calculate them,

and do the same with joy,

victory, union, birth, embrace, dance

and subtract one from the other.

What remains?

Not zero.

Not balance.

But something Søren named:

The Surplus of Suffering.

The residue that remains when you've accounted

for everything, and something still burns.

The one who ascends the throne after the slaughter

of millions feels no joy.

They have merely remained.

Floating on an ocean of the defeated's pain.

Survival, he said,

is not the same as winning.

When a lion rips the throat of a fawn,

there is no triumph.

Only continuation.

Not driven by violence,

but by need.

And behind that need lies the torn body of a child

and the tear-stained eyes of its mother.

So, a question remains:

What does it mean,

when survival itself is so merciless?

Søren found the answer in the silence of the

Buddha:

This existence,

Its very nature is suffering.

Not as an error.

As law.

The *Buddha* said:

The economy of being,

Its currency is pain.

And so his answer was:

extinction.

To step out of the profitless trade of being.

But Søren couldn't accept that.

He wasn't the kind to retreat.

Not from pain.

Not from being.

Not from the story.

Even if suffering was the cost of existing,

existence still had something to say.

He didn't find the full answer in the *Buddha*.

At least not all of it.

The *Buddha* saw pain

but from close up.

Microscopic.

Like someone peering through a microscope:

the individual ache,

impermanence,

attachment,

death,

separation.

But something was missing.

The broader map.

Macroscopic vision.

And Søren found that the map in *Spinoza*.

Unlike the *Buddha*,

Spinoza saw the world from above,

not particle by particle,

but all at once.

Not human suffering,

but the movement of being itself.

From his view, suffering wasn't a cause.

It was an effect.

A consequence.

The *Buddha* had placed pain at the beginning,

but *Spinoza* said the cause was distance.

The nature of existence was separation.

And what fills that distance?

Suffering.

Spinoza understood:

Suffering is not a starting point.

It's a result.

A result of distance.

Distance between things.

Not only between people.

But between everything and everything else:

Cause and effect,

Lover and beloved,

Old age and youth,

Destitution and wealth,

Decay and beauty.

The universe began with a particle,

and distance

was its first consequence.

Not just a concept,

but a movement.

Mechanical.

Unstoppable.

Outward-bound.

The *Buddha* did not see this part.

He sought freedom from suffering.

But suffering is not just born of desire.

Sometimes, it's simply another name for *distance*.

And maybe the answer is not in non-being.

Maybe the answer lies in something more concrete:

In ending the rule of distance.

In persistence, not just survival,

but reunion.

Liberation, Søren thought,

means fighting distance.

And maybe love

is the most visible face of that battle.

It was a freezing Midwestern afternoon.

Søren was driving home after another empty day at the office, before his years in academia.

One of many highways.

He took the exit ramp east, then onto a road tracing the Mississippi River, once called *Mississippi River Boulevard*, a name more romantic than the traffic it carried.

That's when it started.

A strange feeling crept in,

a quiet collapse.

His head grew light.

Not dizzy, but unanchored.

And everything around him, the trees, the sky, the horizon began to fade.

Not disappear.

Just dim.

Like a room with a light slowly turned down.

Only this wasn't the room.

It was the universe.

No. *His* universe.

Søren was dying.

Even in that state, his mind did what it had always done, *calculate*.

Less than sixty seconds, he thought.

Enough time to pull over.

Maybe.

To lie down.

Maybe someone would stop.

No cell phone in his coat pocket.

Only breath.

And numbers.

The car kept moving, he couldn't stop it.

He wasn't steering anymore, though his hands still held the wheel.

To his right, he saw a woman.

Biking along a trail that followed the road.

She was not part of his life.

Not before.

But now, she belonged to what remained of it.

It felt official, somehow.

As if death had begun its paperwork.

He had always believed, especially in those earlier, more devout years.

That when death arrived, he would meet it properly.

He would ask for forgiveness.

Offer remorse.

Reach for salvation.

But none of that came.

Instead, there was only sensation.

He felt himself being pulled,

like a thread unspooling.

Or a whirlpool drawing the center in.

There were only two entities left in the world:

Me and *Not-Me*.

Everything else, the steering wheel, the windshield,

the sound of the tires, the road itself became part of

the same thing.

Not him.

Even the woman on the bike,

not a person anymore, but a symbol.

Part of the fading whole.

And he,

he was what was being released.

Then, Søren turned inward.

To God.

Not with terror.

Not even with hope.

Just this thought:

You finally see me.

Now I am chosen.

He was sure it was ending.

But then…

A shoulder.

The car coasted just enough.

He opened the door.

Threw himself out.

Cold air, rough ground.

He landed on the grass.

Chest rising, barely.

And then she arrived.

The woman from the trail.

She dropped her bike.

Ran to him.

No hesitation.

No questions.

Just help.

Dr. Claire Wittmore's office was modest, tucked above a bookstore in downtown Minneapolis. The walls were lined with shelves, half psychology, half poetry, and a small window cast slow-moving afternoon light onto the carpet. Søren sat on the edge of the couch, his palms resting on his knees as if bracing against memory.

Claire waited. Her presence was steady but unintrusive.

"What stayed with you most from that day?" she finally asked. "Not the facts but the feeling?"

Søren didn't look up. "That I'm separate. Fundamentally. I felt… a kind of final loneliness. The kind that doesn't come from being unloved, but from seeing clearly that you're a distinct thing in a universe that isn't you." He paused. "And also, strangely, I felt seen. Not comforted, not saved. Just… noticed. Like something looked back."

Claire's voice was soft. "You describe yourself as a separate entity. Was that frightening?"

"No," Søren said. "It was strange. But it felt familiar, like I had known it all along and only just remembered. As if I'd been walking beside something my whole life but never turned my head to look."

He leaned back slightly. "Everything else, the sky, the trees, the car, even a woman on a bicycle, became one thing. I was the second thing. And if it had gone further, I think I would've left the body to that first thing and become… soul. Or nothing."

Claire nodded slowly. "You said it felt like a *reminder*, not a *shock*. Can you say more?"

"I've believed for a long time, since I was a teenager maybe, that we already *know* what we are. Not scientifically, but existentially. It's just… buried under stories. We're narrative beings. We don't see reality, we see stories. And the one who tells those stories, the narrator, is built by everything: genes, trauma, gender, class, and history. At the moment of death… the narrator loses control. It couldn't process what was happening. It tried to keep going, but the jurisdiction wasn't its own anymore."

He was quiet, then added: "It didn't die. But it staggered. And when it did, I could see through the bubble."

Claire didn't fill the silence that followed. Søren eventually continued.

"I used to believe in God in a traditional way. Now, it's more like *Spinoza's* idea, God as the structure of reality. That day… I felt that structure looking at me. Not judging. Not saving. Just… watching. Like a teacher who finally notices you. Even if he punishes you, it means you matter."

"And you said something else," Claire prompted. "That *death happens like this.* What did you mean?"

Søren exhaled through his nose slowly. "Death isn't separate from us. It walks beside us like a shadow. It's always in our peripheral vision. We forget it's there and that forgetting is part of how we live. But sometimes, one moment, it steps forward. Becomes the foreground. And when it does, we don't say, 'What is this?' We say, 'Oh. Yes. I've seen this before.' Like a dream, we forgot but always carried."

He looked directly at Claire now. "And the narrator, can't handle that. There's no time to invent a story. It's silent. And that's when we see the real thing."

Claire asked softly, "And now? You survived. The narrator's returned. Has it changed?"

Søren gave the faintest smile. "It's not stronger or
weaker. But now it knows that I know. The
narrator, the one that filtered everything, lost its
sovereignty that day."
He paused.
"And now the narrator? He's still here. Still
weaving tales with flair. Still pretending I'm not
watching. But I am. I've seen what comes when he
falls silent."
He looked toward the window, not at the city but
through it.
"I can't unsee it."

Søren first met death at the age of eight.
Not in the pages of a book.
Not in the hush of a classroom.
Not through a whispered warning on TV.
It came closer than that.
It wore white.
A casket, low and polished,
carried in silence by adults who suddenly seemed
small.

That moment rearranged the furniture in his mind.

His thoughts.

His dreams.

His slow, quiet drift toward what he would later call
belief.

No child truly makes peace with death.

Not at eight.

Not without armor.

Søren was unusually sharp, perceptive in ways that
made him harder to comfort.

He didn't need anyone to explain it.

He understood, too clearly, too soon,

That death wasn't a detour.

It was the path.

And worse, it was universal.

His parents, too, were on it.

But a child's mind can't hold a truth so heavy.

So, it shapes something softer.

And Søren began to shape.

He didn't draw diagrams or write formulas.

What he built was quieter.

A private system stitched from images and ifs.

A personal cosmology.

In this system,

death was not erasure.

It was transit.

People didn't vanish.

They shifted.

Moved from one room to another.

One round closed,

and Søren?

He remained.

Not untouched,

but still present.

The one still watching.

But even this belief had its flaws.

What about the ones he loved?

The ones who kept his world standing upright?

If they left, if their light went out,

what then?

And so, the system evolved.

Each person, he decided, lives in their own world.

A complete one.

Self-contained.

What we see of them is only their reflection.

A trace cast onto our own world.

When someone dies, it is only the reflection that

goes dim.

The person,

in their world,

remains.

That thought,

it held him like a lullaby.

Not a lullaby of truth,

but one of comfort.

And when his grandmother died,

the one who knew how to listen,

the one who held him like a small sun,

this belief is what carried him.

Not the funeral.

Not the grave.

Not the platitudes of adults trying to sound brave.

Just this:

She is gone from sight,

but not from being.

Years later, Søren would whisper to himself.

Maybe none of it was true.

Maybe it was only a shield.

A way to stay upright when the world wobbled.

But the idea never left him.

It folded itself into the quiet of his thinking.

That each of us walks through a personal world,

stitched from memory,

sheltered by meaning.

And that death,

whatever it is,

might be less of an end

and more of a hand

turning the page.

5 VOID

Søren begins to walk.

At first, he thinks he's heading north. Then,
suddenly, he turns east, not because of a sign or a
landmark, but because something deep and
wordless insists that he should turn right. There are
no markers in the landscape.

No path.

No trail.

No structure.

Just space.

Just the suggestion of direction, as if movement
itself carries its own logic.

He walks for hours. Or days. He can't tell. The
concept of time feels slippery here. Eventually, he
realizes something deeper has unraveled.

Direction no longer means anything.

The idea of going north, or east, or back, the whole
geometry of choice, has collapsed. When he turns to
look behind him, the path has morphed into
something else, or nothing at all.

Space folds.

Memory flickers.

Retracing steps is impossible.

He finds himself in a new place. Or maybe it's the same place, revealed more honestly now.

Grey mountains loom above him, jagged and colossal, their outlines more felt than seen. The valleys between them fall away into darkness. The ground is flat and barren.

No trees.

No grass.

No water.

Not even dust.

There is no temperature.

There is no sound.

Yet something cold begins to form inside him. A stillness so complete it becomes sharp.

A strange anxiety sets in.

It doesn't rise like panic.

It seeps in like fog.

He feels as if he's been marooned on a continent of emptiness, alone, surrounded by the ghost of distance.

He continues walking, but the motion is hollow now.

There is no goal.

No forward.

No change.

He is moving inside a perfect loop as if the landscape reassembles behind him the moment he passes through it.

He could walk forever and never leave.

Here, *time has no interest in passing.*

Ageing means nothing.

Søren is caught in an unbroken stillness, a limbo of eternal self-presence. There are no mirrors, no memories, no hands to shake or eyes to meet. Just the silent press of being.

The boredom is suffocating.

Not the boredom of idle days, but of *being untouched by time*, of having nothing to respond to, nothing to resist.

Then, without meaning to, he whispers aloud:

"Even God is not here."

The words vanish without echo.

The sky doesn't change.

No voice answers back.

There is no divine silence.

There is only an *absence*.

He stands still now, no longer walking, no longer
trying.
And then,
he wakes.

The air in his room was warmer than he expected.
His breath felt heavy in his lungs.
Relief washed over him slowly, like light returning
after an eclipse. But it carried something else
beneath it.
A quiet, unresolved sadness.
The dream stayed with him longer than most, not
because of what it showed, but because of what it
refused to give:
No structure.
No form.
No one but himself.
He sat on the edge of the bed; uncertain how much
time had passed. The clock on the wall offered a
number but not a meaning.

What made direction real?

What gave movement purpose?

What turned space into place and solitude into life?

He had no answers. Only the feeling that something within him had been measured and had come up empty.

The room held its silence like a bowl. Outside, Boston moved without urgency. Inside, Dr. Sara Jacob folded her hands in her lap and looked at Søren, not with concern, but with a kind of intellectual reverence. She didn't ask for a retelling. She didn't need one.

"It was a dream of exile," she said softly, "but not from a place. From being itself."

Søren said nothing. His eyes stayed on the stove's small fire.

"You stood in a world that had been reduced," she continued. "Not destroyed, *erased*. The geometry was gone. The narrator? Gone. The coordinates of space and the grammar of time? Collapsed. Søren…

this wasn't just a dream about loneliness. It was a dream of *ontological vacuum*."

He nodded slowly. "It wasn't death," he said. "Even death wasn't there."

"Exactly," Sara replied. "Because death belongs to a system. It's part of the opposites: *life* and *not life*. But this space? It was before opposites. Before narrative. You weren't dying. You were outside the architecture that makes dying possible."

A long silence. Søren didn't flinch.

Sara adjusted her glasses slightly. "Jung believed that the unconscious doesn't always speak in symbols we can process right away. Sometimes, it shows us *archetypal terrain*, places more than stories. Your dream was not a scene; it was a *primordial container*. And that container was empty. That's not chaos. That's the deepest order refusing to speak."

Søren's voice was quieter now. "It felt like even the Self had withdrawn. There was no gaze. No other."

Sara leaned forward slightly. "Which is why it was so terrifying. Not because it was hostile. But because it was pure *isolation without boundary*.

What you encountered was the *unlit side* of the Self. The shadow of the mandala."

He looked up.

"You see," she continued, "in many systems of thought, the Self is imagined as a circle, a center. But what if the Self also has a *dark hemisphere*? A space where wholeness hasn't formed yet. Where structure hasn't emerged, that's where you stood. You were not in hell, Søren. You were in the womb of the unknown."

Søren gave a faint smile. "Womb feels generous."

"Isn't it?" Sara smiled back. "But I mean it precisely. You weren't being punished. You were being *undone*. That dream stripped you of everything your conscious mind uses to orient itself. The ego couldn't narrate it. And the soul, if we allow that word, was suspended between extinction and emergence."

He said, "I felt like a shadow. But not cast by anything."

"A shadow," Sara repeated, "without light. That's profound."

She let that sit.

Then, gently: "You said something about the collapse by the Mississippi River last time. That even if the storyteller could, it would erase you, too. But it couldn't. That's the key. *Something remained*. Søren, what do you think that was?"

He was quiet.

"My guess?" she offered, "It was *witness*. The thing inside you that saw the void felt the collapse and did not collapse with it. In Jungian terms, that's the *transpersonal witness*. Not ego. Not-Self. Something… older."

He didn't respond right away. His face didn't move, but his breathing deepened slightly.

Sara's tone changed, quieter now, like speaking across a great distance:

"And Søren… some never return from that place. They get caught in the void and call it truth. But you woke up. That means something in you said, *'This is not the whole.'* And that, however small, is a movement. A turning. A seed."

The fire popped. Neither of them flinched.

She spoke once more before ending the session:

"I don't think your psyche is trying to destroy you. I

think it's *clearing the ground.* Because something
needs to be built."

Søren used to tell his students, though he was never
sure how much it mattered to them:
"The questions you ask are mirrors of your life.
The quality of your questions shapes the quality of
your world."
And that mirror didn't show you yourself.
It reflected your world.
And Søren, with honesty and a kind of bewildered
reverence, spent his life standing before that mirror.
Each question, he believed, was a kind of waiting.
A sign of absence.
A subtle way of confessing something is missing.
A gap between where you are and where you wish
to be.
Knowledge.
Happiness.
Love.
Peace.
Virtue.

Each begins in the ache of a question.

A question is a cry, a quiet plea from the pain of distance.

And thinking deeply about such questions is not easy.

These kinds of devastating questions don't wait for answers.

They are the answers.

Proof that something in you still moves.

Still wants to know.

Søren's great question,

the one that shaped all the others,

looked simple from the outside:

"Is man greater than life?"

Sometimes, he posed a thought experiment to his imagined students:

"Picture yourself on a distant island.

No society.

No culture.

No mirrors to define yourself by.

No laws to follow or break.

In that solitude, morality loses its form.

No lies.

No betrayal.

No virtues to uphold."

And yet,

some questions survive even there.

Even without others:

The question of death.

The question of solitude.

The question of meaning, or its absence.

These aren't social problems.

They are existential.

In that imagined aloneness, when the waves gently

collide with your thoughts,

taxes, politics, peace, war, none of them matter

anymore.

At this point, Søren would often pause.

"Philosophy," he'd continue, "doesn't answer

death.

Nor does science."

"That's where religion steps in.

At least it gives an answer.

It says:

'You don't die. You shift.

You move from one dimension to another.

You continue, in another world, or by returning.'"

But Søren saw this answer as more psychological
than metaphysical.
Not necessarily wrong,
just crafted like a warm coat for winter,
For when the cold becomes unbearable.
He respected its warmth.
But he doubted the stitching.
To him, death wasn't a passage.
It was a horizon.
He told himself:
"Death is always with us.
It doesn't arrive.
It doesn't begin.
It just is.
In the background of everything we call life."
He thought of a drive he had taken days earlier:
A long road through an open plain,
rain painting the world with silence.
His mind was on the road.
On the curves. On the signs.
And yet,
he noticed things:
a red tractor on the left,
A field of horses on the right.

Details he wasn't looking for but noticed anyway.

Death is like that.

Always on the margin.

Always alongside.

Not to interfere,

just to witness.

Søren deeply believed

that existence had a soul, an inner self.

And if it had a soul,

then one could return to it.

Not by name.

Not by body.

But by rhythm.

By murmur.

By spark.

And when the time came,

he wouldn't vanish.

He would dissolve.

Not into nothing,

but into everything.

Søren was at peace with death,

because there was nothing in his hands to change it.

Anxiety, he believed, arrives

when you have the power to change something
but you hesitate.

Jade, too, was at peace with death,
or better said, she was honest about it.
Perhaps she thought, like *Epicurus*:
"We are never where death is."
Jade had a clearer understanding of life and death
than Søren.
But her clarity didn't come from books or
philosophy.
It came from watching someone gradually
disappear.
At twenty-five, just as her career in aviation was
taking flight,
when she was supposed to be learning about lift,
fuel, and altitude,
her father began to fade.
The diagnosis:
Early-onset dementia in his late fifties.
Rare.
Unfair.
No warning, just small lapses in memory,

confusion,

and a slow erosion of identity.

First, he forgot what day it was.

Then, whom he had called.

Then, where he was.

And eventually, who he was.

Jade lost him twice.

Once, when he became someone, she no longer recognized,

someone no longer truly present.

And again, years later,

when his body finally caught up with his absence.

But it was that first loss that cut deeper.

She once said:

"I lost him when he no longer shared a narrative with our world.

When you can't share a moment and expect it to be remembered.

That's when time loses its shape."

Her father spent his last years in Crete, at her aunt's seaside house,

a stone home near the sea,

where the wind always carried salt and memory.

Jade would often fly there, unannounced,

and just sit with him.

She spoke little.

Because she had learned something most people

never do:

"Words are made for shared time."

And he no longer lived in that time.

Instead, she would look into his eyes.

For hours.

Trying to glimpse the world he now belonged to.

A world with its own gravity.

Silent.

Answerless.

She once said:

"It was the saddest moment of my life,

not because he was gone,

but because he was present,

and unreachable."

In those moments, something changed in Jade.

Something permanent.

She no longer believed that being meant sound,

or that connection required speech.

She began to understand what it meant to *witness*.

And in Søren's dreams,

though they had never met in real life,

she was that witness.

Most mornings, she would wake with the sense

that something important had just slipped away.

As if something had happened

while the rest of the world was still asleep.

Jade never struggled with ennui or lack of meaning.

At least not yet.

Not because her life or job was full of excitement,

for every excitement eventually ends in boredom,

but because she was at peace inside.

That house she saw in dreams,

it was steady.

Not necessarily grand or beautiful,

but grounded.

But the question of *loneliness* remained unanswered

for her.

Not the kind of loneliness that can be forgotten

by drowning yourself in the trivialities of others and

yourself.

This was existential loneliness.

Maybe she thought like *Martin Buber*:

"Real experience only takes form in the presence of
another,
even if that experience is loneliness itself."
There must be someone
who sees your loneliness.
A soul that *witnesses* it.

For Søren, loneliness wasn't a top priority.
Because for him, who believed in personal worlds,
loneliness was embedded in the fabric of being.
Everyone had their own narrative.
Everyone was trapped in their own story.
He often repeated:
"We don't *have* a narrative,
We *are* the narrative."
A narrative sifted from everything we are:
the self.
And this bubble of solitude and drift,
this prison of the self's story,
wouldn't burst,
except by death,
or by something that melted your inner world
into the world itself.

He had tasted this experience briefly during the
collapse by the river.

But about that brief window
called life,
and everything beyond it,
from negative infinity to positive infinity,
All was silence.
What could he say?
He would tell his students, fewer each year:
"Before diving into the *how*,
always place a *why* on everything."
Nietzsche's eternal "why."
And that's where the trouble begins.
Once you ask *why*,
even a small one,
there is no time machine that can take you back.
Inside, Søren was a ruin.
Like every other human being,
he didn't need a trauma to qualify.
Just being was enough.
But even a ruined house
still offers shelter.
Still grants some safety.

Until one day,

you view it from the outside.

And it becomes unbearable.

Søren saw his house,

his inner self, from the outside.

His dream didn't lie:

The house was a full-length mirror of him.

Sometimes grand, open, alive.

Sometimes, a decaying ruin.

His inner houses weren't stable,

but they were alive.

Alive but bruised.

Søren had to see himself from the inside.

And Jade needed someone

who could see her inner self.

From the outside.

Søren had spent most of his life reading and
teaching mathematics.
Once upon a time, he had fallen in love with its
certainty,
the quiet authority of logic, the crisp elegance of
proofs.
Equations didn't argue. They didn't lie.
They ended, cleanly, clearly, then settled into
silence.
And even when they couldn't be solved,
they held their form,
and that was enough for him.
But somewhere along his academic path,
the classroom had become a performance,
and the blackboard, a shield.
He still taught now and then.
But not with the same certainty.
It wasn't the numbers that had changed,
but his understanding of what they meant.
He had come to see that the real world,
the one made of rooms and cities and people,
was not governed by clarity.
It was built on ambiguity.

In mathematics, boundaries were precise.

In life, they were blurred, fading into each other.

That thought followed him like a shadow.

It lingered in his quiet, empty apartment,

trailed behind him in grocery store aisles,

and echoed in that soft space between waking and

sleep.

Perhaps it had all started with the question of death.

With our collective pretense that we know exactly

where it begins.

Definitions were crisp: legal, medical, even poetic.

But in truth, Søren no longer believed such a line

existed.

Where does life end and death begin?

When does wakefulness become sleep?

At what point does the self begin to unravel?

These were no longer academic questions.

They had become personal.

Urgent.

Fifteen days ago, Søren had submitted his

resignation in a discreet email to the dean.

According to the policy, he had fifteen days to

rescind it.

He didn't.

That morning, he woke up to find this email had
been sent to all faculty, staff, and graduate students:

Subject: Farewell Announcement – Dr.
Søren Hussain

Dear Faculty Members, Staff, and Graduate
Students,

I regret to inform you that Dr. Søren
Hussain has decided to leave our faculty to
pursue new opportunities.

Dr. Hussain joined our faculty in 2015 and
has served as a tenured professor in
Theoretical Mathematics and the
Philosophy of Mathematics. Over the years,
he has made significant contributions to our
academic community, securing over one
million dollars in research funding and
successfully supervising 13 PhD and
Master's students.

We thank Dr. Hussain for his dedication,
leadership, and scholarly contributions, and
we wish him the very best in his new
endeavor.

Sincerely,

Dr. J. Scott

Dean, Faculty of Science

Søren muttered something under his breath about
Dr. Scott and shut his laptop.
But in truth, even Scott, rigid and one-dimensional
as he was, wasn't wrong.
New opportunities were indeed waiting for Søren,
impatient and luminous,
ready to introduce him to the most unknown parts
of himself.

They met at a small Arabic café tucked into the
quieter end of Boston, far from the noise of the
university but close enough that the silence between
them still hummed with shared memory.
Elena had chosen the table, in the back corner, near
the window. She already had a cup of cardamom tea
steaming in front of her when Søren arrived. He
looked thinner than usual but more than that,
untethered as if he had left something behind and
wasn't sure what he had taken with him.
She watched him slide into the seat across from her
and didn't speak right away.

Then, quietly but clearly: "You know when I saw the department email… I didn't believe it. No message. No explanation. Just gone."

Søren tried to smile but ended up just lowering his eyes. "I'm sorry, Elena. I didn't want you to get concerned. I'm just tired. Tired is better than retired, you know what I mean?"

She didn't laugh.

"But I'm sorry," he added more seriously. "You've always been beside me through all the departmental shenanigans. And my personal crap. I'm a mess, Elena."

She looked at him, soft, steady. "Søren, everyone's a mess. You just had the honesty not to hide it behind committee chairs and funding reports."

He said nothing, so she continued. "But tired… that's not nothing. That's not just a mood. It's a signal. You used to say the soul sends signals through silence, not words. Remember that?"

Søren nodded faintly.

She sipped her tea, eyes still on him. "Was there something specific? Something that tipped it over from tired to done?"

He looked out the window, then back at her. "Those
are technicalities. I'm in a philosophical deadlock. I
have to resolve it. The job, the title, even
mathematics, they're illusions. I want to jump out
of this dream."

Elena blinked gently. "Søren… You've always
lived in that question. But something feels different
now. Like before, the 'why' gave you purpose.
Now it's become a weight."

He chuckled dryly. "You're so innocently asked. I
cannot be dishonest. I'm trapped in the Nietzschean
why. You know what I mean. The department
crap… that's the how. And you know I never cared
about those. I didn't even apply for the grant this
year. And the chair got mad. I didn't give a …" He
caught himself. "Sorry, Elena."

She smiled, but there was sadness behind it. "You
don't need to apologize. Not for language. Not for
leaving. But when you say 'jump out of the dream,'
do you mean to leave the world? Or finally, step
into it?"

He didn't answer directly. "You know I can't swim.
I'm afraid of water. This time, I want to float.
Nothing happens.

Do you have the patience for a story?

Elena, gently blowing on her cardamom tea, nodded.

"Once upon a time, in an old Indian kingdom, a play was set to be performed, called The Princess of *Kashi*. Since no girls were available, they gave the role to a five-year-old boy, who happened to be a real prince. His mother, the queen, was so charmed by how adorable he looked in the princess costume that she ordered a portrait of him to be painted. Beneath the image, they wrote: The Princess of *Kashi*. The painting was stored away in the palace cellar, and the years passed.

Fifteen years later, the same prince, now a young man, happened to stumble into that cellar and found the painting. He assumed the girl in the portrait was real, about his age, and he fell for her. Fell hard. She was beautiful. Familiar, but unreachable.

He thought about her constantly, so much that he stopped paying attention to everything else. The king and queen became worried. Finally, an old and wise minister gently coaxed the truth out of him.

The prince confessed he had fallen in love with a girl in a painting.

The minister looked at the portrait and smiled. 'My son,' he said, 'this girl... is you. You played the princess when you were five.'

The prince froze. The love vanished instantly, dissolved like mist, once he realized it had all been an illusion."

Søren took a slow sip from his tea and looked at Elena.

"So, my dear Elena... how many Princesses of *Kashi* do you think we've had in our lives?

How many are we still carrying?

And how many more are yet to come?"

Elena let out a small laugh, not mocking. Just surprised. "That's the first time you've made me laugh and worry at the same time."

She leaned forward. "You're not just tired. You're letting go of the ground. Even your language, it's slipping from explanation to poetry like you're translating your life because prose isn't working anymore."

"You want to float," she continued. "You want to trust the water not to drown you, even though your whole life has been about structure and ground and certainty."

A pause.

"And you bring up the story of Princess of *Kashi*, not for trivia, but because somewhere in you, you think you need to leave everyone behind to become whatever it is you're becoming."

Then, more softly: "Are you planning to disappear, Søren? Or are you hoping someone finds you in the silence?"

He looked at her for a long moment. "I'm not hiding. At least not from you. We'll have our monthly Saturday lunch unless you change your mind."

She gave him a look that was half teasing, half serious: "I'm not changing my mind."

He exhaled. "Elena, you know, for a decade, everything has lost its meaning for me. I'm flying to Lisbon in two weeks. For the first time, I'm doing something completely meaningless. Maybe someone: God, the universe, nature, the Matrix, will speak to me."

"And yes," he added with a wry smile, "I know you're now concerned I'm finally crazy."

She smiled back, and this time it was real. "You've always been a little crazy, Søren. That's never been the problem. And no, I'm not changing my mind. You're not getting rid of me that easily."

"Our Saturday lunches stay. Even if you're time-zoning from Lisbon, we'll improvise."

She leaned back, her voice quieter. "And listen, flying to Lisbon without a plan isn't meaningless. It's a question in motion. You're throwing the pieces into the air and watching how they fall."

Then she looked at him with something gentler, more personal. "But promise me one thing?"

He nodded.

"When you land, when you hear that voice, whether it's God or the wind or some street musician who plays something you forgot you loved, you'll send a message. Even just one line."

She smiled. "Something like: 'I'm still floating.'

Or: 'I found the music.'"

He smiled back. "I promise."

Then he reached for the check and slid it across the table toward her. "Now, bill is on you."

She raised her tea. "Fine. But only because you're potentially having a spiritual crisis in a different hemisphere."

Then, quietly, a toast:

"To meaningless flights, unfinished songs, and people who stay in your life even when you try to disappear."

She is already there.

Not quite in the garden.

Not quite in the house.

Just beyond the light.

Watching.

The garden opens below her like a quiet memory.

She sees *him*, not the man, but the *boy*.

Eight years old, maybe less.

Standing still.

To his right, the inn rises. It is tall and dream-born.

To his left, she stands.

She knows she's not quite herself in this dream.

She is not wearing her own body, not speaking

through her own voice.

But she knows: *she is the one beside him.*

The boy doesn't look at her.

Not directly.

But his nearness says: *I know you're there.*

Ahead of them is the glowing house.

Warm windows. Voices overlapping.

Inside: a gathering of souls.

Jade sees faces pass behind the glass.

Some familiar, some not.

All placed perfectly.

Assigned.

The house is full.

And she knows she could lead him inside.

Could show him which room is his.

But she doesn't.

She turns to the north.

Where nothing has been built.

Where the world hasn't yet chosen to exist.

"Go that way," she says.

She feels the words leave her lips like breath, like truth that doesn't need to be understood to be trusted.

"You'll be okay.

I'll watch you.

Until you disappear."

He looks.

She knows how it feels to want to move and be unable to.

To stand at the edge of the unknown and not yet be ready.

She doesn't reach for him.

Just stays.

A still point in his unchosen path.

She doesn't remember saying anything else.

But she remembers the way he stood there.

And how, even in his hesitation, he was beautiful.

Dr. Luc Armand's office in Paris overlooked the Seine, but the river could not be heard from inside. His space was warm, not clinical, mahogany floors, charcoal walls, and low bookshelves that never reached too high. The windows were tall but curtained. His chair was slightly lower than his patient's, and he never took notes.

Jade sat without her coat. Her hands were folded too precisely.

Luc let her sit in silence until she gave him permission to speak, and when she did, without words, he asked:

"Jade… this dream. You said it wasn't like the others. That you remembered it not just with your mind, but with your *body*."

She nodded once.

He leaned forward, hands loose between his knees. "You said something that caught me," he said. "You said, *'I wasn't quite myself in the dream.'* I want to ask: what part of you was missing? And what part was *new*?"

Jade didn't answer right away. Her voice, when it came, was low, steady. "We don't have bodies in dreams. Or maybe we do. I don't know. But I knew the body I had wasn't mine, even at the beginning. I recognized something… off. I was being used. Moved. I was a vessel."

Luc didn't blink. "That's not possession," he said. "That's the threshold. When the psyche stops expressing itself as you and begins to speak through you."

He paused, not for drama, but for alignment. "So, I ask you this, with feeling: when you told the boy to go into the darkness… did you want to say it?"

Jade's mouth tightened. Her voice cracked slightly. "No. I didn't. It felt… cruel. He was just a boy. He looked like he was shaking. I wanted to take him inside, into the warmth. I wanted to hold him. Tell him it was a mistake. But I couldn't. I just… said it."

Luc tilted his head. "So, the words weren't yours. And yet you felt their weight. You felt their consequences. You witnessed their aftermath."

Jade's eyes were glassy but firm.

He continued, quieter now. "Do you have any sense, any intuition, of whose voice it was that spoke through you? Not as a metaphor. As truth."

Jade exhaled. "Even the house, or the inn… I was confused by it. I didn't belong to it, and it didn't belong to me. It was his. The boy's."

She looked down, then back at Luc. "And the sad thing is… I know that boy. He's been in my dreams before. Always younger than the world around him. Always alone."

Her voice dropped to a whisper.

"And a part of me thinks… the woman speaking through me, was *himself*."

Luc's eyes flickered, not in surprise, but in recognition. He sat still for a moment before answering.

"Yes," he said. "That is extraordinary."

He rose from his chair, only slightly, and sat again, closer, but not encroaching.

"If the voice guiding him into the unknown was not separate from him, but a future fragment of his own soul. Then Jade, what does that make *you*?"

She was still.

"Not as a dream figure," Luc clarified. "But as *you*. A woman sitting in my office, waking in Paris, walking the city, touching your own skin. What does it mean that you dream yourself… as the soul of a boy you have never met?"

Jade blinked once. Her body stilled even further, but her eyes moved, searching the floor as if it had spoken.

"I would find him," she said quietly.

Luc did not respond. He only listened.

And outside, the Seine kept moving.

8　THE SOUL OF NARRATIVE

Søren used to say: *"It's all about conversation."*
Not the kind with handshakes and questions about
the weather, but real conversation. The kind that
turns a monologue into a dialogue. That transforms
an asymmetric tie into something symmetric.
To him, the conversation wasn't just
communication. It was *soul work*. A way to build
bridges between two stories, a shared narrative in
place of parallel noise.
"If story is the soul of information," he once said,
"then conversation is the soul of stories."
And he meant it. Sincerely. Dangerously sincerely.
Søren believed in talking to people, yes, but also to
books, ideas, ideologies… and once, even to *streets*.

It happened on the Canadian side of Niagara Falls.
A conference. Late spring. Elena was there, calm,
clever, always watching from just outside the
frame.
They were walking through an old colonial street,
cobbled and quaint when Søren got that particular
look in his eye. The one that said: *a philosophical
detour is about to occur.*

"You know," he began, "this street once stood
between the American revolutionaries and the
royalists. Literally. A street of division."
Elena took a sip of coffee. Nodded, neutral. The
diplomat of caffeine.
"But more importantly," Søren continued, warming
up, "I believe we can have a *conversation* with this
street."
And that was it. That was the line.
Elena choked. Coffee. Nose. Laughter.
They stopped walking. She was laughing so hard
she had to hold her knees.
At first, Søren didn't register it. Then it hit.
"You want to talk to the street?" she managed.
"You, Søren, should go have a long, deep
conversation with Stonehill Mall while you're at it."
He smiled. Big mistake. She took that as
permission.
"Better yet," she said, wiping a tear from her cheek,
"why not ask the mall out on a date?"
"Elena."
"Maybe you'll get lucky!
Søren was already walking away. But Elena wasn't
done.
Oh no.

"Better suggestion, propose to the mall! She's old but rich. Her father funds cosmic narrative modeling or whatever your current paper is about."
Søren kept walking. Faster now.
"You could have kids! The mall and Søren's child would sell ice cream in the parking lot, *with an epistemology stand!*"
He disappeared down the street. Elena shouted after him:
"Don't go, Søren! Let's have a conversation!"

It was one of those days.
Elena teasing.
Søren half-laughing, half-exiled from his own seriousness.
And this was one of his many weaknesses, someone turning his deepest thoughts into punchlines.
But Elena… was the exception.
The conversation was over that day, at least in words. But the laughter stayed.
So did the story.
And somewhere, Søren still believed that even a street, if listened to closely enough, might just answer back.

From minus infinity to plus infinity, it is green.

The mist, soft and scattered, covers everything.

Not dense, not cold.

A mist that dances with the movement of the earth

and erases the boundary between near and far.

On the horizon, trees stand.

Not clear, not vague.

Like memories that haven't yet decided whether to

stay or leave.

A vast lake, stretching as far as the eye can see, but

shallow.

Its water calm, transparent, silent.

Søren stands in the water, knee-deep.

Alone.

Not anxious.

Not at ease.

Nothing is present.

No one is there.

No gaze.

No gazer.

And yet, he is.

And that is enough.

The silence is not heavy.

But it is complete.

He does not look at himself,

but he feels himself,

not from outside, not from within,

but from between.

And he says to himself:

Everything that exists can be divided into two parts:

Me

and Not-me.

The Not-me is here,

the trees, the mist, the water,

and the absence of anyone.

He

stands in the heart of this absence.

And for the first time,

he feels that absence, too, is a quiet form of

presence.

He wakes up.

He remembers the near-death experience by the

Mississippi.

Why does this image return?

His mathematical mind told him that these were not

two points but two vectors.

In opposite directions.

By the Mississippi: from being to non-being.

And in this dream: from the barren void of

nothingness toward this duality...

and perhaps, one night, toward oneness.

Or as the *Upanishads* say: *Advaita*.

The room was dimmer today. Rain brushed the

windows like breath on glass. Søren sat across from

Sara again, this time quieter, but not because he was

lost. He was listening for something.

Dr. Jacob began, not with a question, but a

statement.

"This was not a dream of collapse, Søren. This was

a dream of *return*. Not to familiarity but to

differentiation. You were no longer void. You were

there. And so was the world."

Søren tilted his head slightly like he was hearing

music that hadn't fully arrived.

Sara continued. "The water, the mist, the trees, they

weren't symbols of confusion. They were symbols

of the *threshold*. You were knee-deep in something. Not drowning. Not walking away. Just… suspended. Present. Do you know how rare that is?"

"I felt I existed," Søren said slowly. "And I had a soul."

"Yes," Sara nodded. "That's what shifted. In the previous dream, there was no gaze, no one to receive your being. This time, there was no person either… but there was *context*. The world was *holding* you. Not embracing you. Not defining you. Just… allowing you."

She folded her hands. "This is what Jung called the beginning of individuation, not in the heroic sense, but in the *ontological* sense. You became aware not just of the 'Me' but of the 'Not-me', not as exile, but as a complement. You said: *The Not-me is here.* That's a movement toward wholeness. That's a psyche re-forming its relation to reality."

Søren spoke slowly. "It felt like something had been born."

Sara responded instantly, her voice warm and firm. "Because it was. In dreams like this, the soul rehearses its own reconstitution. You were reborn, not from a mother, but from the *womb of existence itself.* The mist, the absence, the horizon, all of that was the *placenta.* It wasn't confusion. It was *containment.*"

Søren didn't laugh, but something softened behind his eyes.

Sara continued: "You weren't the creator of that world. And you weren't merely a visitor. You were a *participant* in its unfolding. You *felt yourself,* as you said, *not from outside, not from within, but from between.* Søren that is an exact description of what Jung called the *transcendent function,* the meeting point of opposites within the psyche. Conscious and unconscious. Self and world. Me and Not-me."

She leaned forward slightly. "That is the door to Advaita. Not as theory, but as a *felt sense.* The idea that duality is real but also incomplete."

Søren looked at the floor for a long time. "I said something else," he murmured. "That absence is a quiet form of presence."

Sara nodded slowly. "Yes. And you're not the first to say it. Every mystic, every poet who ever stood at the edge of the soul's horizon has said something like that. But you *felt* it. In your body. That's different."

Søren said, "But it's hard to carry it into waking life. Here, absence hurts."

"It does," Sara replied. "That's the tension of this path. When we're dreaming, the psyche speaks in totality. In metaphysical clarity. But waking life is messy. Compromised. The absence we accept in dreams, we grieve in daylight. That's the cost of returning from the dream with insight."

She leaned back slightly. "But that insight has a shape now. It has water. It has air. It has mist and trees. That means it can *hold weight*. Søren, this was the first time you stood not in *nothingness* but in *being with no demand*. The world didn't require anything of you. It simply lets you be."

A long silence passed.

Sara spoke again. "And here's the most important part. In your near-death experience, the storyteller collapsed. In the void, it had nothing left to say. But in this dream… I wonder if it has returned, not to deceive, but to *listen*. I wonder if the soul has found the narrator, and handed it something true."

Søren looked up. "So, it's not a mask anymore."

"No," Sara said gently. "It may still be a mask. But now… it's a mask that *knows it's a mask*. And that's the beginning of wisdom."

The session ended not with words but with stillness.

Not heavy.

Just complete.

She is not climbing.

She is already there.

Not in the sky but in the courtyard below.

Where cloth drapes overhead, and sunlight sifts in like flour.

She knows there are people above her, climbing something impossible.

She doesn't need to see them to feel it.

Their movement is full of urgency.

The kind that rises before it understands itself.

She doesn't join them.

Instead, she waits.

She prepares the table.

Fills cups.

Lays out bread.

Every movement is unremarkable.

Every gesture is exact.

This is not a ritual.

It is *care*.

Someone is returning.

She doesn't know who.

Not exactly.

But she feels the longing.

The weight.

The climb.

She hears the ladders sway above her.

Feels the heat of the sun.

They thought they could extinguish it, she thinks.

They thought they were meant to.

Then,

he comes down.

His face is pale.

Not from fear but from effort.

She sees it in his eyes:

He understands now.

She doesn't ask questions.

She simply reaches for his hand.

Leads him into the shade.

Gives him a cup.

He sits.

She doesn't look for thanks.

He eats.

And she is beside him.

Not as an answer.

Not as a prize.

Just as *presence*.

Dr. Luc Armand never rushed the beginning. His Paris office, dim, earthen, touched by worn leather and late-morning light, offered no clocks, no frames, no distractions. Jade sat across from him, her posture graceful, the stillness around her neither performative nor shy. She had dreamed again. She had come here to speak of it.

"You weren't climbing," Luc said after a long pause. "You were already there."

Jade folded her hands gently. "Yes. I was below. Preparing the table."

His eyes didn't leave hers. "And when you felt them above, climbing with their buckets and their silent hope, did you feel humble, Jade… or essential?"

She hesitated, not out of doubt but precision. "I think… after he failed, I became essential."

Luc nodded. "You didn't climb. You didn't command. But you remained. And when he returned, that *remaining* became something sacred."

Jade's voice softened, shaded by memory. "I remember feeling happy. Cheerful even. At the beginning, I thought, maybe he's climbing for me." She smiled faintly, almost shyly. "That sounds narcissistic."

Luc smiled gently. "No, that's not narcissism. That's gravity. You weren't demanding the climb. You were inspiring it. Sometimes, the feminine in dreams moves nothing, and moves everything."

Jade's smile faded into something quieter. "When he came down, he looked… pale. Not afraid. Just… changed."

Luc leaned forward. "And when he returned to you, not triumphant, not broken, but simply there… did you feel like he had failed you?"

She didn't even blink. "No. I felt… welcomed. Like something had come back to where it was meant to be."

Luc nodded slowly. "Then it was never about the sun. It was always about the table. The cloth. The bread. The cup."

Jade looked down, then back up. "I was waiting for him. I know that now."

"And did you feel like a part of his dream?" Luc asked, voice softer than it had been all hour. "Or like, finally, you were yourself?"

She didn't hesitate. "I was myself."

Luc closed his eyes briefly, in acknowledgment more than conclusion.

"You weren't his vision," he said quietly. "You were his *real*. And maybe, he wasn't just descending back to earth. Maybe he was descending… *toward you*."

Jade didn't answer. She didn't need to.

The dream had already spoken.

Every dream speaks its own language.

Not just in symbols or strange logic,

but in *grammar, rhythm, and tone*.

Sometimes, even its own dialect.

And for that reason,

Søren had never trusted the business of interpreting

dreams.

Not the kind with symbol dictionaries,

Where every snake means betrayal, every tooth

means fear.

Not even the mystical kind.

The ones heavy with omen, archetype, and

metaphor.

His dreams weren't puzzles to be solved.

They were *languages to be understood*.

Each one had its own vocabulary.

And over time,

he began to divide that vocabulary in two.

1. Narrative Words

These were the fluid elements.

The story-glue.

People and places that kept the current moving.

Not anchors, but buoys.

An old friend from a forgotten summer.

A briefcase left unmarked.

A hallway in a city he'd never visited.

They were like conjunctions in a sentence:

... and, but, then...

Necessary for motion.

Not for meaning.

2. Content Words

These were different.

They carried mass.

Gravity.

They didn't always say much.

But their presence rearranged everything around them.

For Søren, they were always the same:

- The *house*

- A *number*

- And the *woman*

The woman had no fixed name. No single face.

Sometimes, she appeared as a teacher.

Sometimes, a nurse.

A bride. A stranger.

Sometimes, she offered food.

Sometimes, only silence.

But always, she brought the same presence:

Unconditioned caring.

A quiet recognition that asked for nothing in return.

Not pity.

Not romance.

Something quieter.

Older.

The grace of being seen without being judged.

She never tried to save him.

She didn't need to.

She simply stood nearby.

And that was enough.

The house, by contrast, was restless.

Sometimes, it was abandoned.

Its windows dark, its staircase fractured.

A structure that felt hollow, aching, wrong.

Other times, it glowed.

Curtains warm, voices murmuring in the next room.

A place that remembered how to hold life.

Eventually, he understood:

The house wasn't a place.

It was him.

Not his past.

Not his future.

But his *inner shape*.

The architecture of his emotional landscape.

And then, the numbers.

Always shifting.

Always sharp.

For Søren, numbers were never just digits.

They were *evidence*.

Proof that some unseen structure still held.

When the world scattered,

a number remained whole.

One night, in a dream, he saw three numbers:

2584, 4181, 6765

Not vague.

Not shifting.

Clear as a print on a blank white page.

He woke.

Wrote them down.

He knew them.

Fibonacci.

Another sign.

Another alignment.

But the meaning didn't lie in the code.

Not really.

Over time, he stopped seeing the numbers as *messages*.

He began to see them as *places*.

Like the number on a door.

Or the distance between two lives.

They didn't explain.

They didn't resolve.

They simply stood there.

Still and waiting.

Like the woman.

Like the house.

Like the language of dreams itself:

Uncertain.

Unfinished.

And entirely his.

But the language of Jade's dreams

was smoother,

like her own soul.

In most of her dreams,

two elements always returned:

a house,

and the faceless man.

The house,

sometimes small, sometimes vast,

sometimes rustic, sometimes modern,

always held a sense of presence.

It was a place where something settled,

like silence folding itself into the heart of light.

No one knew

whether the house was inside Jade,

or inside someone else,

or simply the manifestation of a nameless longing.

But the man,

he had no face,

yet his presence was undeniable.

No voice, no name,

but when he appeared in her dreams,

he brought faith.

Though he seemed unsure.

He didn't quite know that he knew.

Jade felt that the man carried a beautiful soul.

Whenever they were at altitude,

his fear wasn't of falling,

nor of gravity's cruel pull,

it was of suspension,

of that uncertain middle,

between letting go and holding on.

The man carried something within him.

that Jade couldn't look past.

Not because of love,

but because of a kind of understanding.

It didn't feel like an answer.

It felt like an invitation.

In the dream, he is alone in his house.

Not just his current house.

Though parts of it are there.

The stairs are the same.

The kitchen feels familiar.

But the rest...

belongs to other times and places.

Fragments of his childhood home,

hallways he hasn't walked in years,

doors he remembers

but hasn't opened in ages.

And then, unfamiliar spaces:

Corners and passages from no life he's ever known.

And yet,

he feels a sense of ownership over it all.

As if it's his.

What unsettles him isn't the collage of architecture.

It's the silence.

He, somehow, understands that no one else exists.

Not just in the house.

In existence.

No neighbors,

no traffic,

no distant airplane in the sky.

Only him.

And yet,

something stirs inside him,

not fear,

but a quiet pressure.

A voiceless call:

Go to the basement.

He doesn't know why.

He simply begins to descend.

The stairs are narrow, a little steep, but intact.

No rot.

No dust.

The railing is made of old wood.

Worn but sturdy.

The light has a deep yellow hue.

Not sickly,

but warm,

like the color of a memory brought into view.

When he reaches the bottom,

he finds himself in the basement of his childhood
home.

It's there,

the back door,

the small rectangular windows.

But they're open.

A breeze drifts through them.

He pauses.

How did I get here?

He remembers the stairs.

But his childhood home never had stairs to this
space.

There was never a way in from inside the house.

He gently closes the windows.

Pulls the door shut.

Something inside him says:

Leave through this door and return through the
front.

And so he does.

But as he crosses the threshold,

something inside him shifts.

He tells himself this is where I should be afraid.

He opens his mouth to scream.

But,

he isn't afraid.

Not really.

There's no one to scare him.

Nothing chasing him.

No presence lying in wait.

Only silence.

And the feeling that

silence isn't emptiness.

It's just complete.

And then,

he wakes up.

The light in Sara's office was softer than usual. The rain had ended earlier that morning, leaving the windows dappled with a drying sky. Søren sat across from her, shoulders quiet, not tense. But something in his eyes said: *I came back from somewhere.*

Dr. Sara Jacob didn't speak immediately. When she did, her voice was slow, grounded.

"This dream is different. Again."

Søren nodded. He didn't need to be told.

Sara continued: "It brings us not into the wilderness, not the mist, not the void, but into *your house*. Or what your psyche calls your house. Familiar and unfamiliar. A collage."

He said softly, "A collage of memories."

She smiled faintly. "Yes. Memory-made architecture. Childhood stairs. An old kitchen. Unknown corridors. And a basement."

Sara folded her hands. "You were called to descend. And you did. That's significant. But you didn't stay. You left. Through the back. And now you say, you don't remember returning."

Søren looked down. "I got scared. I wanted to leave. I just… stepped out. I think I've stepped out of every house I've ever dreamed of."

Sara sat back, absorbing. "Yes. You've always left. Always at the moment, something could be known."

She waited, then asked:

"Søren… do you think what you feared in the basement was something in it? Or was it what the basement showed you *about yourself*?"

His answer came slowly. "I don't know. I told you before… I have this friend, Lana. I've never seen her. But she could see me. Once, she told me: *'You have monstrous power trapped inside. It could destroy or create. But you'll have to face it someday.'"*

He paused.

"I told her I couldn't look inside. Not yet. I don't know what I'd find. I don't know what would be released."

Sara didn't interrupt. She just listened.

"And there's more," he said. "One time, I told her I felt like a fish in a bowl, sitting at the bottom of a lake. I said, 'I just need to swim to the top of the bowl.'"

He looked up at Sara. "And she said, *'There is no bowl. That's only your imagination. You just have to free yourself.'*"

Sara's face didn't move. But her voice deepened.

"That's not a metaphor, Søren. That's a soul speaking through the veil."

She leaned slightly forward, not urgently, but with reverence.

"She wasn't dismissing your pain. She was trying to show you the illusion. You imagined the bowl as a barrier. But she saw it as *belief.* You thought freedom meant reaching the top. She knew freedom meant *realizing the bowl was never there.*"

Her gaze sharpened slightly, not aggressive, but piercing.

"And yet… you told me today, *'I can't go down unless I know there is a soul there.'"*

She paused, letting the weight of that rest between them.

Then:

"Søren, the soul doesn't *wait* in the basement.

It *descends with you.*"

A long silence followed.

"And if there's a monster there," she said, more gently now, "it may not be an enemy. It may be your soul *twisted by neglect.* Waiting in the dark. Waiting for you to name it."

Her voice, barely above a whisper:

"You don't need to be fearless.

You just need to be *willing.*"

The room held its stillness like an understanding.

And the soul, wherever it was, was listening.

13 I WILL VANISH WITHOUT HER EYES ON ME

He is standing in a garden.

The air is cool. The silence is full.

To his right, the house rises, the very inn he's

wandered for what feels like years.

But this is the first time he sees its *exterior*.

It's tall and pale, almost silver in the moonlight.

Still.

As though it wasn't built but *grown*, shaped by time

and memory, not bricks or labor.

To the left: darkness.

Not empty. Just the absence of light. Like a canvas

waiting for form.

But not entirely.

A *woman* stands there. Half in shadow.

Long black hair.

Calm. Beautiful.

Familiar in the way that dreams remember you

before life does.

She doesn't speak.

She doesn't move.

But her presence pushes back the dark.

She is a stillness he recognizes but cannot name.

Then, the shift.

Now he is *eight years old*.

The woman beside him is the same.

Her presence unchanged.

No flicker, no blur, just her.

Ahead of them is a *house*, larger than any he's ever seen.

It glows from within.

Every window is lit.

Inside: a celebration.

He sees people through the windows.

Some faces he knows. Others he's never met.

And yet, each one feels *assigned*.

Like the house is solving itself, one soul per room.

Every room is full.

Every variable is assigned.

Except him.

The woman beside him doesn't point to the house.

She turns instead toward the north.

There is *no house there*.

Only night.

But not even night, *something deeper*.

A path that disappears into blackness, darker than dark.

Un-rendered.

"Go that way," she says.

Her voice is quiet.

No fear.

No doubt.

"You'll be okay.

I'll watch you.

Until you disappear."

He wants to step forward.

But he doesn't.

He looks at her.

She doesn't push.

Doesn't plead.

She just waits.

And the waiting is love.

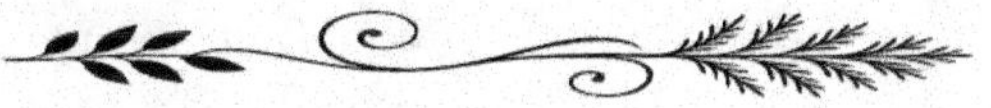

The fire in Dr. Sara Jacob's office had burned low. Just embers now, soft, red breath in the cast-iron stove. The rain tapping the window sounded like a clock without hands.

Søren sat in silence, his expression somewhere between grief and recognition. Sara didn't press. She simply began.

"This dream is different," she said. "Not because it's less strange. But because you are no longer alone in it."

Søren looked up, eyes tracing a memory not yet language.

"You've seen the house before," she continued. "Many times. But this time, you're outside of it. For the first time, you saw its exterior, silver in the moonlight, still tall. As though it had *grown*, not been built."

Søren nodded slowly. "It didn't feel like mine," he said. "It felt like… me. Or, more disturbingly, my inner self. My soul. And I had been… abandoned from it."

Sara met his gaze with calm precision. "Exactly. The house is not your possession. It is your psyche. And standing outside it means disidentification. The Self is showing you its own image, its own structure, from the outside in. Not as a mirror, but as a monument."

Søren was still.

She went on. "And then the woman. She was not new, was she?"

"No," he said quietly. "There's always the woman. Sometimes with a face, sometimes not. But always present. And always… safe."

Sara nodded. "This is your *Anima*, Søren. In Jungian language, the woman in your dreams is more than feminine. She is the soul's bridge to the unknown. The intermediary between your inner world and its mystery. In early dreams, she appears as a stranger, young, radiant, unknown. But as the psyche matures, she often becomes a mother. Not just your literal mother, but the *archetypal mother*. The one who contains the origin."

He closed his eyes for a moment. "She didn't change. But I did. I became a child. Eight years old. She was still the same."

"And that," Sara said softly, "is profound. She is eternal in that dream logic. Her constancy is not realism, it's *truth*. The timeless feminine presence that accompanies you, across age, across form."

Søren opened his eyes. "But then came the part I can't forget."

"Yes," Sara said. "The house full of light. The glowing windows. Every room assigned. Everyone with a place. Except you."

Søren didn't speak.

Sara let that breath live, then continued:

"And instead of pointing you toward the warmth, toward the known. She turns toward the north. Toward darkness. Not even night. Something before night. And she says, *'Go that way. You'll be okay. I'll watch you. Until you disappear.'*"

Søren's voice cracked, not loudly, but along its edges. "That's the part that shattered me. I felt… I exist only as long as she can see me. That I vanish without her gaze."

He swallowed. "You remember the void dream. I said I didn't have a soul there because there was no other soul to reflect mine. And here she confirms it: *'I will watch you until you disappear.'*"

He paused.

"Logically," he added, "the truer sentence might be: *'Until you disappear, I will watch you.'* As if she knows her limit. She cannot preserve me. She can only witness."

Sara didn't interrupt.

Her voice, when it came, was low and sure.

"Yes. That is the pain behind the beauty. The love she offers is real but not rescuing. She will not walk with you into that blackness. She will not lie. She names the truth: that her vision has a boundary. And beyond that, you must go alone."

She leaned in, not physically, but emotionally.

"Søren… you've just named one of the most ancient fears in the human soul. Not loneliness. Not death. But *unwitnessed disappearance*. The fear that if no one is looking, no one loving, no one remembering, then you don't just go unknown. You *cease to be*."

His hands were folded tightly now. Not in prayer. In containment.

"And what makes it so holy," Sara continued, "is that she doesn't plead. Doesn't command. She simply *waits*. And her waiting is love."

Søren's shoulders loosened, barely.

Sara's voice softened to a whisper.

"You haven't disappeared, Søren. You are here. And I see you."

The rain outside paused for a breath.

And for a moment, so did time.

The apartment in Athens was just as she remembered it, sun-bleached curtains, neat corners, the smell of lemon polish and oregano. And the quiet. That particular kind of quiet that only mothers can cultivate: one-part order, one-part judgment, one-part worry.

Jade sat on the edge of the living room couch. Her bag was still by the door. She hadn't even taken off her shoes.

"I was in Crete last June," she offered gently. "It was hot. I visited my cousins. Helena is getting married."

Her mother emerged from the kitchen, wiping her hands on a towel. Not angry. But armed.

"Of course, she is. Helena's always been practical. Not floating in the clouds like some people. She knows what matters."

She sat across from Jade. Her eyes softened but only slightly. "And what about you, Jade? Still, flying airplanes instead of building a life? You're almost thirty-eight. You should be a mother to two children by now, not circling the world alone."

A beat.

"What happened to that nice Greek boy? Andreas, the one with the publishing business? Did you scare him away, too?"

Jade exhaled, voice tightening. "Do you want to start again? I'm here to see you. Why can't we have a normal mother-daughter relationship?"

Her mother sighed. Sat down, slower now. "I do want that, *agapi mou*. But every time you come, it's like you're already halfway out the door. You want normal? Then tell me what normal is in your life. Flying across continents, no husband, no home, no church. No one to come back to except me, and you barely even do that."

Then, more gently: "I'm not trying to fight. I just… I don't understand you anymore."

Jade looked down. Her voice was sharp but cracked. "You know what, Mom? Dad was right. Instead of judging people, try to understand. This is my life. Not yours."

That name. That invocation.

Her mother stilled. When she spoke again, her voice had lost its edge, but gained something else: a fracture.

"Your father was always too soft on you. He let you believe being different was a shield. But the world isn't soft, Jade. And neither is time."

Her hands curled slightly in her lap. "You think I don't try to understand? I brag about you to my neighbors. Captain Jade Galani, I tell them. First female pilot on whatever route. Even when I don't understand you, I love you. But you treat me like a checkpoint. Like love is just tolerating me for two days before you disappear again."

A silence fell. And Jade broke it, softly, devastatingly.

"Do you want to know why I stayed away?" she said. "Do you really want to know?"

Her mother looked at her. Bracing.

"Because Dad died alone."

The room stopped breathing.

Her mother's voice fell, brittle and thin. "Don't… Jade, don't say that to me."

"You think I don't know that?" she said. "You think I don't carry that with me every night? He left without a word. He went to silence and never came back. And you, you never came back either."

Tears rose now in both their eyes.

"He died in silence," her mother whispered. "And I've been living in it ever since."

Then she looked at her daughter, not as a parent, not as a critic, but as a woman who had been left behind.

"You never asked how I survived it. You just ran. And now you come back to tell me how wrong I am… when all I ever wanted was *you*."

Now, it was Jade's turn to break. The tears came, unannounced, unguarded.

"I'm sorry, Mom. I didn't mean to bring back old wounds. I'm here for two days. That's all. You can come to Paris if you want. You're retired now, right? Your brothers are there too. If you can't tolerate me, at least be near your family."

Her mother's face shifted, somewhere between pain and disbelief. Then she rose slowly and came around the table.

"I don't want to be close to family," she said. "I want to be close to you."

She sat beside her daughter, her voice trembling.

"I'm tired too. Not just in my bones. Tired of pretending I don't miss you in every room you're not in. Tired of protecting my pride instead of reaching for my child."

She placed a hand over Jade's.

"I don't care if you never marry. I don't care if you never go to church again. I just want you to come home and not feel like you have to defend every breath you take."

They sat like that, two women with all their defenses finally stripped away.

Jade sniffled. "What do we have today, Mom? Any food from Crete? I just missed those days."

Her mother smiled, small but unmistakably warm.

"Of course, I made something. What do you think this house has been waiting for?"

She disappeared into the kitchen.

"I made *Dakos*. And *Boureki*, just like your aunt used to make. And *Koulourakia*, too, even if you still pretend you don't eat sugar."

Jade let out a wet laugh.

Her mother returned with a tray and set it gently on the table.

"I didn't know you were coming," she said, "but something in me… did."

Then, softer:

"If you say you missed these days… then stay for all of them. Not just two. Stay until the food runs out. Stay until the silence doesn't feel like a wall anymore."

She reached for a plate.

"Eat, Jade mou. You're home. At least for now."

15 THE COMPOSER OF HIS OWN SILENCE

Søren is back in Tehran.

Not as memory renders it but as it lives in a soul untouched by time. The cracked sidewalks, the scent of damp dust rising from old stone, the low murmur of traffic folding into the evening call to prayer. It is a city breathing inside him, and he walks it with a strange, solemn joy.

He finds his way to the building where he once worked, the mathematical research institute, its plain facade familiar and unassuming. Inside, the light is yellowed, softened by age, and yet the laughter of his old colleagues makes the air feel young.

They welcome him without ceremony as if he had never left. They pour tea in thin glasses, crowd around worn tables, pulling out notebooks filled with equations and open questions. They speak of recent papers, of stubborn conjectures, of absurd stories from their younger days. The laughter comes easily, fuller than he remembers laughter could be.

As evening thickens into night, someone suggests
he stay in the guest unit upstairs. His flight to
Boston is at nine the next morning.

The guest house is simple, with a narrow bed, a
lamp that buzzes faintly, and a window overlooking
an empty courtyard. He leaves his bag by the door
and goes to the small reception area. A woman at
the desk, warm-eyed and unhurried, assures him
they will wake him at 5:00 AM.

"Don't worry," she smiles. "Sleep well."

Relieved, light, Søren returns to his room. The
mattress sags a little in the middle. It doesn't matter.
Sleep pulls him down fast, like gravity in an old,
forgiving world.

But something shifts.

The sense of a body on a bed dissolves. The
window, the night air, the coming flight, all vanish.
Now, Søren is not inside himself. He is outside.
Watching.

A conference room unfolds before him, sterile and
colorless, as if painted from a palette of fatigue and
resignation.

The lights hum softly overhead, casting pale halos
on the worn wood of the table. Three figures sit

together. Their white coats gleam faintly, catching the thin, uncertain light.

Dr. Amini folds his hands, fingertips pressed together and looks across the table at Dr. Bahrami. "Doctor Bahrami," he says, his voice even, almost measured, "please begin your full report on the patient's current condition."

Dr. Bahrami straightens slightly. A heavy file rests before her. She speaks clearly, without rushing.

"This patient, Søren, whose full name is Sorena, chooses to call himself Søren, after the Danish philosopher Søren Kierkegaard. Philosophy, particularly Existentialism, defines his identity almost more than mathematics does.

He was once a prodigy. He won a gold medal at the International Mathematical Olympiad as a teenager. His doctorate is in Philosophy of Mathematics from *Georgetown University*. He returned to Iran and accepted a faculty position at the University of Tehran.

Approximately fifteen years ago, Søren appears to have suffered a nervous breakdown. It went unnoticed. There were no family members no close friends able to intervene.

Five years ago, he admitted himself voluntarily into our institution.

He claims to have a child, a daughter most often, sometimes a son. The daughter bears different names at different times: Leyla, Sonya, and Gita. The son remains unnamed. Based on his own timeline, this child would now be between thirteen and fifteen years old.

However, exhaustive research confirms Søren has no children. No marriages. No known long-term relationships.

And yet, he speaks of the child not with delusion, not as a hallucination, but as a logical anchor within a consistent, internal world.

Moreover, Søren demonstrates extraordinary cognitive function. He remains capable of immediate numerical categorization, particularly within sequences such as the Fibonacci series. Incidentally, the room numbers of his so-called 'friends' correspond precisely to Fibonacci values.

Initially, Søren financed his own institutionalization. When those funds were depleted, an unknown benefactor continued paying

for his care. We have no official record of this
person.

Another pattern has emerged with equal clarity.
Søren believes, persistently, without deviation, that
he has a flight scheduled for Boston via
Amsterdam. This belief has been continuous for
five years.

Every evening, he arranges for a wake-up call.
Every morning, he prepares to leave. The flight
never comes. He never boards. Yet the ritual renews
itself, day after day, like an endless rehearsal for a
departure he cannot name.

His so-called friends, colleagues he claims worked
with him years ago, share this alternative reality
with him. Their conversations, their jokes, their
research problems, all synchronize perfectly within
his narrative.

It is not merely a personal delusion. It is a *grand
narrative*, a shared architecture of existence.

And I must confess," she pauses, "sometimes, when
I sit with him... I wonder: how is their grand
narrative any less valid than ours?

Where does our certainty come from? From
repetition? From consensus?

Søren's world is internally complete, recursive, and coherent. Ours may only seem more 'real' because we have agreed not to question it."

She lets that hang in the air for a moment.

"There is one more behavior I must highlight. Søren exhibits an intense and ritualistic relationship with music. He will listen to a single piece on endless repeat, not for comfort, but to sustain his inner architecture.

Last week, he played *Secret Garden's Passacaglia* continuously, day and night, for almost four days. The staff had to remove his phone charger to interrupt the cycle. Even then, when the battery finally died, he seemed to emerge from a trance, dazed but somehow... relieved.

The looping of the music mirrors the looping of his life: the child, the flight, the friends, the numbers. He is not seeking escape. He is composing survival."

In the end, I must mention one more thing, perhaps it seems minor.

Søren has two heroes he often spoke of:

Job, the prophet, and Prometheus from Greek mythology.

The first accepted his narrative, even though he did not understand its meaning.

The second rebelled against it, and in doing so, became aware of its meaning.

And I believe Søren, in the end, chose the path of Job.

She ends this last sentence with a sympathetic sigh…

And closes the file.

"That concludes my report."

The room holds a delicate silence.

Dr. Amini sits back slowly. His eyes, dark and sharp, settle on her as if weighing something that cannot be fully spoken.

"You have done well, Dr. Bahrami," he says at last. "You have seen deeply."

He leans forward, voice dropping slightly.

"This is no ordinary psychosis. This is a construction. A world built against the collapse of meaning."

He taps the table softly with one finger.

"Flight. Friends. Child. Music.

Each one is a pillar.

Each one holding up the sky."

Dr. Arad glances up from his frantic notes.

"But... Doctor," he stammers, "if his world is complete... if it holds its own logic... how do we know he's the broken one?"

Dr. Amini turns to him calmly.

"We do not."

A long pause.

Then, back to Bahrami.

"You asked the correct question," he says. "What separates his grand narrative from ours?"

He smiles thinly, not unkindly.

"Only inertia. Habit. Fear.

We cling to our reality because it comforts us.

He clings to his because it saves him."

He rests his hands flat on the table.

"So. We face a choice.

Do we tear apart the tapestry he has woven?

Or do we bear witness?"

He waits, not impatiently.

Dr. Bahrami speaks without hesitation:

"I witness him."

Dr. Amini closes his eyes briefly, then nods once as if accepting a private truth.

"Good.

No interventions.

No dismantling."

He glances at Arad.

"And you, Arad, enough writing. Learn to listen."

He stands, smoothing his white coat as if sealing the

agreement into the fabric of the day.

"You are his witness now, Dr. Bahrami."

The room breathes again.

But the deeper work, the real seeing, has only just

begun.

Søren had seen that dream more than three months

ago,

and for days afterward, he lived beneath its shadow.

The last time he had been in Tehran,

he was eight years old.

The day he left it behind for good,

flying toward America with his parents.

Though the opinions of others had never truly

anchored him,

he spoke of the dream to no one.

Neither to Sara nor to Elena.

In a quiet moment, it crossed his mind:

perhaps this path of self-destruction

had already sealed off any way back.

Two weeks before resigning from his university

post, Søren sat alone in his office,

wondering which preceded the other,

the world of dreams or the world of waking.

Of course, he didn't consider either of them *real*.

Not in the ordinary sense.

Not when he sensed a hidden order in both,

yet felt how differently their rules applied.

In the waking world,

which he preferred to call *the sensory world*,

the laws of physics ruled:

Gravity, acceleration, light, matter, the body.

But in the dream world,

those laws had been excused from duty.

There,

if gravity existed at all, it arose from fear.

Movement, if it occurred, pulsed from desire or

dread.

Ladders hung from the sky

without anchoring to anything.

And if you leapt,

you didn't fall.

Unless waking had taught you that you must.

Søren saw dreams as a domain of primal emotions,

the kind Paul Ekman had once listed:

joy, anger, fear, surprise, sadness, shame, contempt,

pride, disgust.

Emotions planted in us before language,

before logic,

before any civilizing lesson.

And this alternate order

brought him back to a question that had lingered for

years:

If a dream is an image of waking life,

could waking life be an image of something else?

He called that something *the realm of awareness*,

not self-awareness,

but a layer above all this,

like the veils of an onion folded into each other,

or curtains fallen over deeper curtains.

He had no conclusive proof,

and made no grand claims.

He knew well the idea was unfalsifiable.

But his inductive mind kept nudging him:

If once, the correspondence between dream and

waking occurred,

perhaps it will happen again.

Perhaps it's happening even now.

But how would this higher realm be governed?

Not by physics.

Not by chemistry.

Not even by time.

If there were laws,

they might be of meaning.

Of presence.

Søren saw himself again,

in a classroom with empty chairs,

standing before the board, a piece of chalk in hand.

He had drawn a cylinder on the blackboard.

He would say:

If light shines from one side,

its shadow becomes a rectangle.

If it shines from above,

the shadow is a circle.

Dreams, he thought, worked the same way:

Shadows cast from something more complex,

falling across the screen of emotion.

In dreams, gravity becomes fear.

And now, his question was no longer about dreams,

nor about waking,

but about what stood behind both:

What is the cylinder an image of?

He is surrounded by people.

They move with rhythm, exchange glances, and pass tools from hand to hand. A kind of silent choreography holds them together. It feels organized, but improvisational, like jazz.

He recognizes none of them.

Except two.

A quiet man his age whose presence feels like a reflection. And a woman, young, confident, warm. Her voice carries laughter, and her eyes are dark like night water. She speaks sparingly, but every word arrives like déjà vu.

Together, they are part of something. A mission, though no one explains it. The urgency is shared. Someone needs help.

Maybe it's my mother, he thinks.

The plan is strange.

But everyone accepts it.

They collect *ladders* from alleyways, from old barns, from behind forgotten shops. Wood, aluminum, splintered, gleaming, every kind imaginable.

The group stacks them together.

A rising chaos of intent.

They build a staircase to the sky.

"To extinguish the big candle," someone says.

He almost smiles.

But then he looks up.

It's not a candle.

It's the *sun*.

And they are carrying *buckets of water*.

He climbs with them.

The sky deepens.

The ladders sway.

The wind rises.

Each rung feels thinner than the last.

Each breath, a wager.

Still, he climbs.

No one questions how high.

No one asks what happens next.

The world below becomes small.

Abstract.

Irrelevant.

He is afraid.

He has not been this afraid in years.

But it's not death he fears,

It's the absurdity of the quest.

And yet,

he climbs.

Until the sun is just above him, immense and

untouched.

There is no flame.

No wick.

No candle.

Only *light*.

Untouchable.

Unmoved.

The water he carries feels ridiculous.

The group is silent now.

They see it too.

There is nothing to extinguish.

Søren is the first to descend.

The fear does not vanish.

But it softens.

Becomes understanding.

He returns to the ground.

And *she* is there.

The woman with her calm eyes and dark curls.

She says nothing.

But she *knows*.

She takes his hand.

This leads him to a covered space, part courtyard,

part kitchen.

A table waits.

Steam rises from cups.

Bread glows golden in a bowl.

She serves him. Without ceremony. Without words.

He sits.

He eats.

And in the quiet presence of her care,

he understands something he cannot name.

The light moved differently in Sara's office that
morning, cool but not distant, like memory on glass.
Søren sat with his hands open, not in restlessness,
but in readiness. A stillness had settled over him,
but not one born of peace. It was the stillness that
came after climbing.

Sara waited for the room to breathe around them. Then, she began.

"Søren… this dream isn't about the absurdity. It's about what came after it."

He didn't respond at first. His mouth opened, then closed. Finally:

"I knew it wouldn't work, even before the climb. We were carrying water to extinguish the sun. There's no logic in that."

"No logic," Sara agreed softly. "But there was something else. What made you climb anyway?"

Søren looked past her toward the corner of the room. "Duty. Maybe pressure. But mostly… because the group believed. And I didn't want to ruin that. Everyone was so certain. It felt… sacred, even though it was insane."

She leaned forward just slightly. "So, you climbed not for the outcome but for *their belief?*"

He nodded. "Yes. I think that's when something changed in me. I realized... even if I knew it was impossible, it wasn't mine to shatter."

A pause. And then his voice softened:

"I once told someone I believe in the idea of

believing in belief. And *Tarkovsky*, he's my all-time favorite filmmaker, he understood this."

Sara didn't move.

"In the final scene of *Nostalgia*," Søren continued, "the protagonist, Oleg, is told to walk across an empty pool carrying a lit candle. He's told it might save the world or fulfill a madman's prophecy. He doesn't believe it. He doesn't even fully understand it. But he sees the devotion in the man who does. And so, Oleg walks."

Sara stayed silent.

Søren's voice didn't tremble, but something inside it cracked. "He walks across the pool, slowly, carefully. And the candle stays lit. And the world doesn't change. But something *true* happens."

He looked at Sara. "That's how I felt in the dream. I climbed not to reach the sun but because I couldn't betray the sincerity of the people around me. Especially the scared ones. Especially the quiet ones. Especially... her."

Sara finally spoke. "Her."

"She was there," he said. "The woman. She had a face this time. Warm eyes. She didn't speak. Just waited. And when I came down, she took my hand.”

Sara nodded slowly. “She didn’t reward you. She didn’t comfort you with words.”

“No,” Søren said. “She fed me. Bread. Steam from a cup. And she sat with me.”

“What did it feel like?” Sara asked. “That moment at the table?”

Søren’s eyes glistened. “Like the universe finally gave me a hug. Like it bent its head, not because I succeeded, but because I tried.”

Her voice softened even further. “And that… is not love in the way we use the word. That’s *presence*. That’s the sacred feminine, not rescuing, not fixing, but *receiving*.”

He nodded.

Sara leaned in. “What you found at the top of that climb wasn’t a lie. It was light. Untouchable. Real. But not extinguishable.”

She paused.

“And when you came down, you were met not by philosophy. Not by explanation. But by care.”

Søren didn’t speak.

"You cracked something," she said gently. "You didn't fall apart. You opened. And what poured in wasn't certainty. It was kindness."

He whispered: "That's why I couldn't tell the others. About the sun. About the candle. I descended in silence."

"And that," Sara said, "was your rite of passage." She held his gaze.

"Some people believe they have to fix the world. Others think they have to destroy the false beliefs in others. But the wisest… the wisest protect the storyteller. Not because it's true. But because it holds the soul together, until something deeper is ready to emerge."

Søren's eyes dropped. He inhaled sharply. "She doesn't know my name. And I don't know hers."

Sara smiled faintly. "No. Not yet. But the dream remembers both of you."

And outside, unseen by either of them, the sky remained bright.

Unafraid.

Unbroken.

And unextinguished.

Søren had a habit of reading almost all major scriptures.

But he approached them in an unusual way:

He would read *as a believer*, even though when he finished, he made no commitment to live as one.

It wasn't about conversion.

It was about engagement.

He believed the only way to truly understand a sacred text was to step fully into its world while reading it, to get involved with it at full emotional and intellectual capacity.

Only after finishing would he step back, reflect, and decide what, if anything, stayed with him.

When he read the *Bhagavad Gita*, which he grew to love deeply, he didn't worry about what really happened with Arjuna.

He didn't argue about the historicity of the events.

It wasn't important to him whether they had happened exactly as described.

He assumed belief temporarily, like putting on a lens, so he could grasp the message without resistance.

That, for Søren, was what he called *having a
conversation with the scripture.*
(Although, as he joked to himself, he wouldn't dare
tell Elena that, she would surely find a way to turn
it into another public comedy show.)
Søren believed you couldn't have a real
conversation without a *shared discourse.*
You had to meet the story where it stood, not from a
place of skepticism but of temporary trust.
From that simple decision, everything else opened
up.
He never wasted time arguing about miracles, how
someone could part a sea or how a virgin could give
birth.
Those were distractions.
The truth was always between the lines.
You read as a believer, then you took a step back:
If the message resonated with your soul, you keep
it.
If it didn't, you moved on to the next text.
Simple.

Later, Søren began thinking more seriously about the nature of *faith* itself.

What was it?

He realized that, surprisingly, the *subject* and the *object* of faith were not the most important parts.

It was the *relationship* that mattered most.

He often gave an example:

Imagine two absolutely unbearable people, selfish, rude, unpleasant, and yet, somehow, they loved each other deeply.

You might not like either of them individually, but it didn't mean their love was worthless.

In fact, Søren would say,

"I respect that love, even if both of them are complete assholes."

He saw something sacred in the *connection* itself.

The same way, he hated when, for example, a mother, out of hatred for her ex-husband, would try to sabotage the relationship between father and child.

In Søren's mind, this wasn't just personal cruelty.

It was a *betrayal of the sacred relationship* that existed between a parent and a child, something larger than personal anger.

Faith, he believed, worked the same way.

It was not just faith in God, or truth, or scripture.

It was *faith in the relationship itself.*

And Søren, dangerously and stubbornly, believed that faith in the relationship was sometimes even stronger, and more important than faith in the thing itself.

Søren's struggles weren't always existential.

He, like anyone made of bone and blood, had ordinary sorrows too.

The worst year came after the collapse by the river. Not just the physical fall, but everything that followed. New city. Career shift. Friends lost to time and distance. And then, in the span of nine months, both of his parents were gone.

He didn't show it.

He rarely did.

He played strong, moved like stone, and laughed at the right moments. But inside, he was a wineglass wrapped in paper.

Fine.

Cracked. Held together by work, and more work, and more work.

No one broke his heart. He did that himself.

He could complain, but he knew he was his own most dangerous opponent.

His story, if it could be called that, couldn't be told without his parents. They brought him here without his permission, and the toll was this: to watch his childhood vanish like a snowball left beside a fire.

They were good people.

But different.

His father was secular, full of humor, ideas, and longings.

His mother was sacred, steadfast, faithful, flame-lit.

They stayed married.

Perhaps they shouldn't have.

Perhaps they did it for him.

Cut-and-paste love.

A compromise made permanent.

Søren didn't inherit their beliefs.

He inherited their contradiction.

He became a sailor, drawn by currents both spiritual and unsatisfied.

His father was the wind. His mother, the beacon.

One pulled him forward, to uncharted waters. The other called him home.

But the wind never brought him to shore, and the beacon never moved.

He still remembers a dream, fifteen years ago.

A desert road, long and bare like Nevada. A fork ahead. Left or right.

He knew what right meant: safety, home,

predictability. Buy the house. Marry. Have children.

Life is a straight line.

He called it "the tradition."

Left was something else.

Wilder.

A tattooed wonderland.

Flight lessons.

A motorcycle.

Too many lovers.

Ambitions stacked like towers.

Startups.

Scholarships.

Risk and thrill and ungrounded stars.

And still, fifteen years later, he stands at the fork.

No closer to deciding.

Still listening to wind and light, pulled between

velocity and warmth, longing for a map in a world

made only of weather.

He is already there.

Standing at the edge of something ancient. A pool, but not one built by hand. It's carved from the bones of the earth, surrounded by silence and faint echoes of movement from deep within.

He stares at the water. The edge is safe, clear, cool, and inviting. But a few steps forward, and the bottom disappears. Darkness swells beneath the surface.

And he remembers: *he never learned how to swim.*

Not in water. Not in this.

Whatever *this* is.

Others leap without pause. Boys, maybe men, diving and rising like the world has no weight.

Their laughter doesn't touch him. It's distant, like a memory from someone else's life.

He dips a foot in. Then more.

And suddenly panic.

Not from drowning. From *not understanding*.

He backs out. Fast. The wet stone underfoot almost slips.

Then she is there.

She enters the water like she belongs to it. Hair slicked back, eyes calm, not demanding, not forceful. Familiar.

He doesn't know her name. But he's seen her. A dozen times. A hundred. In corridors. In light. In rooms without numbers.

"You don't have to know how," she says. "I'll show you."

He almost believes her.

Almost.

But belief has never come easily.

He steps back again.

And she doesn't chase him.

She stays in the water, glowing slightly in the dim.

A fixed point in something vast. She isn't disappointed.

She just waits.

And he wonders if next time he'll stay.

He doesn't follow her.

Just watches as she slips beneath the surface, smooth, silent, certain.

The water closes over her without sound.

He stays on the edge.

Not ready.

Not yet.

The silence returns.

But something remains.

A trace in the air.

Sandalwood. Cedar.

Not perfume.

Not artificial.

Something older.

Earth and smoke.

Wood warmed by the sun.

He closes his eyes.

He doesn't know her name.

Doesn't know why her voice still echoes beneath his ribs.

But he remembers the scent.

And for some reason, that feels like enough.

The room was quiet, the kind of quiet that arrived before words and lingered after them. Søren sat across from Sara, eyes calm but not settled, like a surface that had just been touched. He had already shared the dream: the stone pool, the dark water, the scent of sandalwood and cedar. Sara had listened with her whole body.

Now, she began to speak.

"You didn't run from fear," she said gently. "You stepped back from something more dangerous: *Uncertainty*."

Søren nodded slowly, hands folded. "I wasn't afraid of drowning. I was afraid of losing control, losing form. I need predictability. I like logic, mathematics, and cities. Even in meditation, I don't go past a certain point, I don't want to let go."

Sara tilted her head. "That pool wasn't just water. It was an unstructured being. No edge. No certainty. No frame."

He exhaled. "The edge was safe. The light hit it right. But it disappeared fast. I put a foot in, and then, I panicked. Not because of danger. But because I didn't understand."

"And then she appeared," Sara said, her voice low.

"Yes." His voice softened. "She didn't force anything. She moved as if the water belonged to her. Calm. Familiar. She said, *'You don't have to know how. I'll show you.'* I almost believed her."

Sara watched him carefully. "But you didn't step in."

"I wanted to. But I felt something pulling me back. I trusted her… but I didn't trust myself. I thought if I go in, my darker forces might surface. The ones I keep under control. I felt her presence couldn't hold them."

Sara nodded slowly. "You feared not what she would do but what you would become."

He didn't respond right away. Then: "Yes."

"You weren't afraid of her," Sara continued. "You were afraid of being unmade in front of her."

Søren looked down. "I told you before… form is both my device and my prison. It holds me. Holds my soul. Lana once said: *"It's just your fishbowl."* And she was right. But I can't crack it. Not yet."

There was a long pause.

Sara asked, "When she slipped beneath the surface… and you were left alone… what did you feel?"

Søren's voice was quiet but precise. "Both. Regret that she wasn't there to see me. That I lost my witness. But also, a relief. No more pressure."

"You hate pressure," Sara said.

"I do."

"She didn't demand anything. She waited. But her waiting itself… was a kind of invitation."

He nodded. "Yes. That's the part I feared most. The possibility of trust."

"And if she had waited a little longer?" Sara asked.

"If she had stayed just a few more breaths…, do you think you might have stepped in?"

He was still. Then:

"I think so."

Sara said nothing.

The silence in the room became the water.

And for a moment, the edge felt less like a boundary,

and more like a place to begin.

19 THE SPACE AND THE MOMENTS

The air is cool and echoing.

Cave light flickers across the water's surface, the walls breathing with a silent rhythm.

She stands near the edge of the pool, the stone beneath her feet, smooth and damp.

The water is clear and still, shallow at first but darkening fast, falling away like a thought you're afraid to finish.

To her left, young men are diving in.

Joyful, weightless.

Their bodies disappear into the deep and return like seals.

She watches them. Watches one in particular, *him.*

He stands apart.

Not near the others.

Not even close to the water. Just near enough to feel its presence like a question waiting to be answered.

She knows he's afraid.

Not of the water itself but of what it might ask from him.

For a moment, he takes a step forward.

He enters. Just barely.

And then retreats.

She doesn't say his name, she never does in dreams, but she walks calmly into the pool and lets the water surround her like trust.

"It's all right," she says gently, her voice like light underwater.

"You don't need to know how. I'll show you."

He shakes his head.

She sees it in his eyes, logic battling instinct, fear wrapping itself in the language of caution.

She reaches toward him, but not too far.

Not to pull.

Just to be there.

"You're not alone," she says.

"I'm here. I always have been."

But he steps back, and the water parts.

She doesn't follow.

She just waits.

Jade sat across from Dr. Armand in his quiet Paris office. She was composed, but not distant. There was something tender in the way she held her knees together, hands resting like petals in her lap. She had dreamed again.

Dr. Armand listened without interruption.

When she finished, he waited a few moments, then said, "You weren't dreaming for yourself," he continued. "You were dreaming through yourself. The water wasn't yours. The fear wasn't yours. But you entered it anyway."

"I felt responsible," she said. "At first, I was just… joyful. I wanted to swim. The water was beautiful, dark but clear. But when I saw him…" she paused, "it changed. I felt something shift inside me. Like I was sent there."

Luc tilted his head. "Did you think he was afraid of the water?"

Jade shook her head. "No. He wasn't afraid of drowning. He was afraid of… *what the water would take from him,* of losing his structure. He's a man of logic. Of form. In water, there's no shape. I think that's what scared him."

Luc didn't blink. "He whispered numbers, you said."

"Yes," she replied, her voice softer. "That's how I knew he was even more abstract than I first thought. He was holding on. That was his anchor."

He nodded slowly. "And you… you entered without needing an anchor."

She looked away for a moment, then said, "I told him, *'I'll show you.'* I meant it. I thought he would trust me."

"And when he stepped back?" Luc asked gently.

"I wasn't hurt. I wasn't rejected," she said. "I understood. I was afraid I had embarrassed him… in front of the others. The young men diving like dolphins."

Luc's voice became quieter. "So you didn't want to rescue him. You didn't even try to follow him. You just… waited."

"Yes."

He let the silence breathe, then asked, "And when you said, *'I've always been here,'* did you understand what that meant?"

She shook her head. "Not really. I said it in the dream. But I didn't plan to. I didn't even know what I meant."

Luc leaned back slightly. "That's why it was true."

Jade's gaze was distant, thoughtful. "Sometimes I'm afraid I'll stop dreaming about him. I don't know why. I don't even know who he is."

"You've seen him before?"

"Yes," she said. "But the first time… I wasn't even me. I didn't have a body. I just knew he was there. And every time he appears, the space belongs to him. The inn. The ladders. The pool. None of it is mine. But the moments… they are mine."

Luc's voice became more intimate. "You said you don't believe in soulmates."

"I don't," Jade replied. "But maybe… eyes. Recognition. If he exists in the real world, I would want to meet him, not for answers. Just to stand in front of the questions."

Luc said nothing for a moment. Then he spoke softly, with great care.

"I wasn't asking if you believe in soulmates," he said. "I was asking if you believe in *being prepared*."

Jade looked up.

"Sometimes the dream doesn't ask us to find someone," he said. "It asks us to *become someone* so that when the moment comes, we know how to hold it. Not because it answers anything. But because it reminds us who we already are."

She didn't reply.

She didn't need to.

The dream had already been answered for her.

It was early afternoon in late autumn of the previous year, overcast skies hung above the university campus. The maple trees had shed most of their leaves. Sonya had knocked on Søren's office door, holding a worn folder and visibly anxious. Søren, buried in papers, had half-expected another excuse about deadlines. But when he saw her, something in her face, the quiet tension, the tired eyes, had stopped him.

Sonya had been a brilliant undergraduate, top of her class, driven and sharp. But she had always remained reserved about her personal life. Søren had seen something of his younger self in her: the solitude, the intensity, the quiet weight of thought. He had often treated her like a daughter in spirit, respectful but quietly protective.

When Sonya mentioned needing an extension, Søren had initially prepared to question her sincerity. But then he had seen her fingers tremble slightly as she held the folder. Her words had been steady, but her voice had carried weight, not laziness, not manipulation, but grief.

He had gently put down his pen.

Instead of pressing, he had offered,

"Let's go get a coffee. I skipped lunch. My treat."

In the quiet corner of the campus coffee shop, over warm drinks and the sound of soft jazz playing from the speakers, Sonya had opened up for the first time. She had shared what she'd been carrying:

-   The sudden disappearance of a lover she had trusted.

-   A father who had left when she was young, unreachable even now.

-   A mother trapped in bitterness and blame, directing her pain inward.

Sonya had been overwhelmed. She hadn't told anyone else. And Søren, though unprepared, had become her only listener, perhaps the first one who had truly heard.

Sonya, quietly, eyes on the table:

"I know this wasn't how you wanted to spend your lunch break. I'm sorry."

Pause.

"It's not really about the deadline, Dr. Søren.

I mean, it is, technically, but... I think I've been

holding too much. And now it's leaking into everything. The project. My sleep. My body."

She swallowed hard.

"I didn't think it would hit me like this.

He left.

Without a word.

Not even a text.

And I thought I was smarter than this, that I'd never get pulled into something so… helpless. But I did."

A long breath.

"It's not just him. It's like... something opened.

My father left when I was nine. Just vanished into another life. A different country. I don't even know where.

And my mother… she never forgave him.

Not once.

She wears that bitterness like a second skin. It covers her and speaks for her. She doesn't even see me anymore.

And I think, I think I became good at school to make up for something. To build a shelter out of numbers and logic.

But now? Even that feels… unstable."

She had finally looked up at Søren. Her voice was steadier but raw.

"I'm tired of being brilliant.

I just want to be allowed to fall apart for a minute. To be unreasonable.

Would that be okay?"

"First of all, don't forget the protocol, I'm Søren, not Dr. Søren.

Second, yes, especially this time, it's okay. You have every right to be unreasonable. I understand that.

Let me tell you a story about one of my favorite professors. When I was doing my Master's, I went through a somewhat similar situation. I had my defense exam scheduled, but all of a sudden, due to some stupid paperwork issue, the department canceled it. My life crumbled. I had to move back home. I had already terminated my roommate agreement. I was literally homeless.

I knocked on the department chair's door; he was also my favorite professor. I was angry and heartbroken. Half a broken heart, actually, because yours is whole. And I want to respect your pain. That was the year I had just started smoking. When

I stepped into his office, I said, 'Professor, I have to smoke in your office.'

And he said, word for word:

'For this special time, you can be unreasonable.'

So yes, it's okay."

Sonya, with a small, disbelieving laugh, her eyes suddenly misting:

"You said that just now, *you have the right to be unreasonable*, and something cracked in me. No one's ever said that before. Not my mother, not my professors, not even myself."

She wiped a tear quickly, embarrassed.

"And this story... Søren, I mean, thank you. Really. That moment in your life, it's like I can see it. You are standing there with a crushed heart, a crumpled housing contract, and a lit cigarette like some rebel philosopher mathematician… and your professor didn't tell you to toughen up. He just made space."

She nodded slowly.

"I needed to hear that.

Because everything in me is trying to hold it together, to be rational, elegant, and composed, in the same way I try to write proofs.

But pain… it doesn't respect structure. It leaks.

Breaks the form. Multiplies.

And I keep trying to contain it in clean lines and

due dates."

Her voice softened, almost a whisper.

"But I didn't want to be perfect right then.

Just real.

And maybe even seen.

Søren … thank you for seeing me."

"Okay, then we agreed, you could be unreasonable

for a while. But, like everything, there's a deadline.

After that, you go back to reason.

As for the project, I could give you an extension.

But to be fair to the other students, you'd have to do

some extra work. We could talk about that later.

Maybe we could even submit the paper we'd

discussed in class.

But for now, forget about school.

Do you remember what I once said in class?

'We are the narrative, but we live under the illusion

that we are the narrator.'

Do you remember that?"

Sonya, a slow, grateful smile forming through the

weight on her face:

"Yes… I remembered.

You said it on one of those strange days, half the class was lost in their phones and half in existential dread. You closed your notes and said,

'We are the narrative. But we live under the illusion of being the narrator.'"

She paused, the words clearly landing again, fresh.

"I hadn't understood it fully then. Maybe I still don't. But lately... it rang louder. Like I was watching my life unfold like a movie I had been handed a ticket to, but not the script. I kept trying to rewrite the scenes as they played out, but maybe that was the illusion. Maybe I was just a character trying too hard to edit the film from the inside."

She looked at him almost pleadingly.

"But Søren, what if the narrative hurts? What if you don't like your role?

Or worse… what if no one's reading?"

Her voice cracked again, not dramatic, just soft truth.

"Sometimes I felt like a paragraph that had been left out of the book."

Then, after a pause, more gently:

"But maybe that is why we need other readers.

Other witnesses. To remind us that the story is still

being written. That we still matter on the page."

She held his gaze, quieter now but clearer.

"And that day… you reminded me of that."

"Yes. Once we realize that we are not the narrator but the narrative itself, we are left with two choices, there is no third.

Either we accept our narrative, even if we don't understand its meaning,

or

we stand against it, like *Prometheus*.

Acceptance, which is what Stoic philosophers often teach, is similar to the concept of Dharma.

Do you know what *Dhamma* is?

Dhamma, or *Dharma* in *Sanskrit*, is an ancient word.

It means the truth of the way things are.

Not just rules.

Not duty like we usually think.

But more like the pulse of the universe that runs through us.

The order of our being.

Our role in the story even if we haven't written it."

He paused, watching her eyes search the air.

"To accept our *Dhamma* is to live in alignment with

it,

like a tree growing toward the sun,

even if it doesn't know what sunlight is.

That is one path: *stoic*, quiet, faithful.

We bear the weight without asking why every five

steps."

He leaned forward now, more serious.

"The second path is resistance.

The Promethean path.

We steal the fire.

We refuse the script.

We say: 'No, this isn't my story.'

But Prometheus is chained to a rock, Sonya.

And every day, the gods send an eagle to devour his

liver.

He chooses pain over submission.

Meaning over peace.

Creation over comfort."

He let that settle.

"You asked what to do with a narrative that hurt.

The answer is cruel but honest:

You either carry it with grace,

or you burn trying to rewrite it.

And some of us,

most of us,

spend our lives caught between the two."

He looked at her.

"Where are you, Sonya?"

Sonya sat quietly for a moment, then exhaled

slowly:

"So…

Either I carry the pain like it is mine.

Like I have chosen it.

Or I stand up and scream against it, knowing I'll

bleed for it."

She ran a hand through her hair, half-laughed

without joy.

"You make it sound noble.

But both choices feel like losing."

Looking down, her voice softened.

"I think I have been pretending I am strong enough

for the first one,

the carrying.

But I was angry.

Not just at him.

At everything.

At the way people walk away like love was

something disposable.

My mom, who is too busy hating my dad, doesn't
notice I was falling apart.
And professors who say 'life happens' and still
want a ten-page proposal."
She glanced at him.
"Present company excluded."
She wiped under one eye but didn't cry.
"Maybe I have been Prometheus without realizing
it.
Just quietly getting eaten day after day.
And the worst part?
Nobody even know I am chained."
After a pause.
"You said we were narratives.
Maybe mine is broken.
Maybe that is why I came today.
To ask if I am allowed to throw out the pages and
start again."
"First of all, accepting your narrative actually
requires more bravery, honestly. Because most of
the time, we don't even know what we are being
punished for.
But if you ask me, I'd say you should reject your
narrative. Say no. Just like Prometheus said no to

Zeus.

But it wouldn't be easy.

Acceptance means staying in the silence.

Rejection means walking into the silence, into the dark, with no fire left because we have already given your fire to humanity.

I am not a therapist, thank God.

And I am not a neuroscientist.

But I can share my own experience, how I changed the narrative."

Sonya leaned forward, her voice hushed but intent: "Yes.

Please.

Because at that moment, it feels like I am living in a story I don't write yet can't escape.

And worse, one I don't even understand.

I think I have been waiting for someone to give me permission to say no.

To not just carry the pain but to push back."

She looked up, her eyes clear now, if still a little weary.

"Tell me how.

Tell me how you changed your story."

"Let's start with something a little absurd.

Just the professor in me trying to turn every moment into a lesson for one of my most brilliant students.

Then I'll give you something practical.

The first idea comes from the linguistic relativity hypothesis. I mentioned it once in class; you might've missed it. It suggests that the language we speak actually shapes the way we think about reality.

In its strongest form, it even claims that learning a new language can rewire the brain.

I tested this in class once. Maybe we'd talk about that experiment later.

But here was a funny story. A friend of mine have once been upset with me. I wrote her an email in my native language, Farsi. It came out poetic, sad, and full of nostalgia, and all I had been doing was apologizing.

Then, I rewrote the email in English. And suddenly, it was sarcastic. Lighthearted. Even a little comical.

Why? Because each language carries its own narrative.

It was eye-opening.

I even tried learning a new language, *Sanskrit*.

Not the wisest choice at my age. Too slow.

Anyway, before we go deeper into the next point,

let's order your coffee. And your favorite donut.

Then we'd keep going."

Sonya cracked a faint smile for the first time, her

voice soft but amused:

"Sanskrit?

Seriously, Søren?

You just had to go for the most ancient and

complicated one?"

She exhaled a hint of laughter behind the tiredness.

"But that's beautiful.

I mean.

The idea that each language carries its own soul...

Its own narrative gravity.

I'd never thought of it that way."

Then, playfully.

"Okay, professor.

Let's do your sacred ritual. I'll take a black coffee,

no sugar.

And the donut?

Chocolate glaze. No shame."

She lifted her eyes to his, the humor now touched

with something gentler.

"Thank you… for this.

For being unreasonable enough to sit with me

here."

"I'm glad you brought up the soul. Yes, I do believe

language carries its own soul.

Even though I lean toward *Chomsky's* idea of

Universal Grammar, I can't quite resist the thought

that each language brought its own inner life."

He paused, then shifted slightly in tone.

"Now let's move to something more practical, and

don't worry, it doesn't require learning Japanese,

Mongolian, Arabic, or Turkish."

He leaned forward.

"Here's what I mean:

Try becoming a witness to your narrative, not a

victim of it.

Step back from the story and take hold of the

narration.

Be real, not delusional.

You aren't helpless in this.

Try writing your memoir. But in third person.

As if you are observing yourself, not judging, not

justifying.

Just watching.

Watch your pain.

Listen to it.

But don't whine. Don't dramatize. Just witness.

Does that make sense?"

Sonya nodded slowly, her eyes fixed on the rising

steam from her coffee:

"Yes…

I think I did."

She paused, her voice more careful now like she

was testing the weight of each word.

"You are saying…

instead of drowning in the pain,

I write it.

Not like a diary, not like 'I feel this, I feel that,'

but as if I'm watching someone else live it."

She looked up at him.

"Like a film. Or a novel.

'She sat across from her professor, coffee

untouched,

heart loud in her chest, trying not to cry.'

Like that?"

She held his gaze now, her voice steadier.

"If I do that…

Maybe I stop being inside the spiral.

Maybe I can see the shape of it.

Maybe… I can find the thread that leads out.”

Then, almost to herself, soft and real:

“You are the first person who asks me to witness

my pain,

not fix it.

Thank you, Søren.”

After coffee and pastries, they began walking

toward Søren’s office.

Søren, and perhaps later Sonya too, knew that what

he had offered her was no remedy. It was no cure

for pain. It was simply a lullaby. A gentle one.

Søren had learned it from a book.

A form of meditation.

To observe his thoughts, his temptations, his anger,

and his wounds not as a participant but as a witness.

To sit with them.

To listen.

Søren could even reduce physical pain using this

method.

His explanation was this: part of the pain, beyond

the nervous system, is our narrative about it.

The storyteller in us wants to weave a tale around

the ache.

Unfurl its history and geography before us like a map.

But if we take the seat of the narrator, the entire setup dissolves.

Still, Søren knew well:

Changing one's narrative is nearly impossible.

But what exactly did Søren mean by *narrative*?

Was it not extreme to claim that we are nothing but our stories?

In Søren's view, a human being had two parts:

The *soul* is abstract, immutable, and bound to Being itself. He sometimes called it the *inner*.

And then, the *narrative*, what he also referred to as one's personal world, the sum of everything that situates a person in the fabric of life.

In this framework, the soul was bound by the narrative,

and only in rare moments, such as profound insight or unmediated encounters with existence, like the threshold of death,

could it slip free?

Søren had experienced one such moment by the river that day.

He believed the structure of the narrative was triangular:

- *Conditions*: what is given before us and outside our control: genetics, gender, class, culture, history, geography, and family.
- *Decisions*: choices that appear to be ours.
- *Chances*: events neither sought nor foreseen.

Søren's view leaned toward determinism but not fatalism.

He saw free will as an illusion, an idea shaped by his personal reading of Stoic thought and *Spinoza's* philosophy.

So, while decisions and chances seemed to stand apart from conditions, he believed all three were interwoven in a vast chain of cause and effect.

The only difference lay in how visible they were,

Not in their nature.

Perhaps the only trace of freedom that remained was in how we face our narrative.

That was the one thing he had offered Sonya:

the ability to stand in the narrator's place.

Even then, he wasn't sure it was truly possible.

Because even if one believed in choice,

as Søren often said,

the architecture of the narrative remained intact.

What was clear, at least, was this:

Conditions and chances lie beyond our command.

And all our effort, all our striving,

is to make our decisions a little more conscious.

And lessen, as much as we can,

the weight of the other two sides.

Søren's silence was a musical one.

Not absolute silence,

absolute silence had no form.

To him, it resembled the barren dream of pure

nothingness, the void.

But music would arrive, offering him a blank

canvas.

A frame.

Like a mother's lap, generous, unwavering, reliant.

And in that, he could remain forever, silent.

Music was one of the rare things that carried soul in

mathematics, but took body in physics.

And he used to say this often in class:

"If we need just one proof of Descartes' greatness,

it's the grandeur of music."

Music had a soul.

And that soul was abstract, timeless, formless.

Its soul was mathematics.

But its body lived in the physical world,

in sound, in frequency.

Perishable, compound,

subject to the hands that played it.

But what remained eternal,

was the soul of music.

Music was sacred to him because it connected him

perhaps like *Leibniz* (whom he preferred over

Newton) once said:

"Music is the pleasure the mind experiences from

counting, without realizing it is counting."

Once, on a train ride back from a conference in

Oslo, he sat by the window and listened to

Schubert's Serenade on loop.

Music was like water

and he let it quietly take him in.

Søren avoided suspension.

But the only kind of suspension he welcomed

was being submerged in music.

A trance, like *Nirvana*.

Like that last drag of a cigarette before you stub it

out.

Deep.

He let the trance of music envelop him,

because he trusted it.

The same way he trusted existence.

Because he believed sacred mathematics slept

beneath all of it,

beautiful yet precise, like a clean equation.

And he let the universe take him in,

despite all the pain within it.

If the universe wounded him, and it often did,

He had nothing else to cling to but the universe

itself.

Like a child scolded by his mother,

who still runs to her arms,

because there is no one else to dry the tears.

And music, in all its beauty and magnitude, would

make him weep,

and be the one to wipe his tears.

And Schubert, in that dull train ride,

did just that.

That was the last time he cried in public.

No sobbing. No shaking.

Just quiet, unshaken tears.

Later, in a dream,

when he touched a window that wouldn't let him

through,

and when that woman crossed it,

a phrase from that *Serenade* rose quietly in his

chest.

Not in the form of sound,

but in the shape of ache.

But Jade could sit with pure silence.

She may have even enjoyed it.

Her inner world was calm. Undisturbed.

The mirror of her questions never revealed anything

too complex.

And that didn't bother her.

Jade's struggle was with the soul.

A soul in search of a witness to her solitude.

And had she, like Søren, come to know the soul of

music,

perhaps she would have seen

that the soul of music is the best witness to a lonely

and soundless cry.

But even Jade, the agnostic,

was drawn to the magnetism of music.

It was spring, in Prague, years ago.

She had a long, unscheduled stopover on her way to

Moscow.

Forty-eight hours.

She wandered through narrow alleyways,

sunlight draping the rooftops in waves of amber.

And then she heard it,

a pianist,

at the foot of a church staircase,

his fingers falling on the keys softer than a spring

drizzle,

a melody unfolding and curling with impossible

grace.

Someone whispered:

"It's Chopin's Spring Waltz."

The pianist was not famous. It wasn't a formal

concert.

He was simply alive.

The music had soul, unapologetic, radiant,

yet never brash.

There was a fire in it.

A quiet laughter.

A restrained joy that cracked her chest open.

She stood at the edge of the square.

Five minutes passed. Then ten.

And when she finally turned and walked away,

she felt lighter.

In her dreams,

when that man grew hesitant,

when his silence sank too far inward,

Jade would sometimes imagine that melody behind
him,

as if her soul had learned to dance

while her body was still gasping for breath.

He is standing in line.

He doesn't know for what.

Or for how long.

Only that it matters.

And that he is not alone.

A woman stands beside him.

He doesn't recognize her.

Not from life.

But her presence is calm.

Steady and still.

Familiar in a way that defies logic.

She says nothing.

But she is with him.

Not just beside.

But woven into his silence.

Behind them stands a boy.

Ten, maybe younger.

Dark curly hair.

Headphones over his ears.

He nods slightly,

not to anyone, but to something he hears.

A melody.

Soft. Circular.

Almost a waltz, but not quite.

No lyrics.

Just rhythm.

Wistful. Haunting. Beautiful.

Søren listens.

The music pulls at him.

Not his ears, something deeper.

He leans back, subtly.

Tries to catch more of the sound.

More of its shapes and contours.

A memory?

No.

A *longing,*

aching to be named.

He mumbles. Quietly.

Just loud enough for the boy to hear.

Just loud enough for the mother.

"I'll find that music one day…"

Neither responds.

The boy doesn't look up.

His mother says nothing.

But Søren glances at the boy's screen,

just in time to see a glimmer of text:

Happiness in the Rain

The phrase lodges in him.

Not as a title.

As a feeling.

He repeats it silently.

Once.

Then again.

Happiness in the Rain.

The woman beside him turns slightly.

Not fully. Just enough.

Her voice is soft.

"Find the music," she says.

"Life is short."

Søren looks at her.

He sees her.

Not a visitor.

Not a stranger.

The song.

The phrase.

The presence.

They are the same.

The light in Sara's office was dim yet warm, with late afternoon filtering through the blinds like the last lines of a lengthy book. Søren sat back in the chair, not relaxed, not restless. Just still. The kind of stillness that only arrives after a collapse that didn't kill you.

He had just shared the final dream.

A line. A woman. A boy. A song. And a phrase that refused to leave: *Happiness in the Rain.*

Sara didn't speak at first. The silence draped around them. Smooth like velvet.

"You weren't searching," she said finally. "You were waiting. And for once, that was enough."

Søren's voice was soft, uncertain. "It felt like a passport office. A small room. But something in the air told me it mattered. That it wasn't random. That it was... sacred, somehow."

"And she was beside you," Sara added.

"Yes," he nodded. "She fills space. She always does. Even when she's not there, her absence feels... full. But in this dream, for once, we had the same mission. We weren't connected by story or name. Just by presence."

"And the music?"

He looked down, as if the memory had weight. "It wasn't loud. Just enough to pull me. Not my ears, something older. The boy had headphones on. He wasn't performing. He wasn't even aware of us. But he carried something I needed."

"What did you feel when you heard it?"

"Longing," Søren said. "Not nostalgia. Not recognition. Something rawer. I mumbled: 'I'll find that music one day.' It wasn't a plan. It was a vow."

Sara was quiet, letting it unfold. "And then you saw the phrase on the screen."

He nodded again. "'Happiness in the Rain.' It didn't feel like a song title. It felt like a key. To something I didn't know I'd locked."

"Did it feel like a memory?"

"No," he said. "It felt like a memory I haven't lived yet."

Sara's voice dropped. "And when she turned to you. When she said, *Find the music. Life is short.*
What happened in your body?"

"I froze," Søren admitted. "Not out of fear. Out of clarity. Because I knew she wasn't giving advice. She was giving me... permission."

He paused.

"I don't believe in soulmates," he continued. "Even Plato got that wrong. But I believe in harmony. There are souls whose rhythm matches yours. Not because they complete you. But because they... compose you. They write the parts you forgot you were meant to play."

Sara didn't move. Her voice softened to near silence. "So, you don't believe in soulmates. But you believe in being seen as music."

"Yes."

She waited.

"And you said something else," she continued. "That you resigned. That you let go of your position. The known. The structure."

Søren exhaled slowly. "I finally listened to Lana. She said there was no fishbowl. And I believed her. I couldn't pretend anymore. The form I lived in, it wasn't safety. It was surveillance. The worst prison is the one where you're the guard."

Sara nodded. "And you were the most disciplined guard I've ever met."

"I broke it," Søren said quietly. "It's already broken."

"And what do you carry with you, now that you've left it?" she asked.

He was silent for a long time.

"Maybe nothing," he said. "Everything belonged to the architect. The one who built the prison. But maybe... faith. Not the kind I can name. And the awareness that I'm alone."

Sara didn't correct him. She didn't soften it.

She just let it be.

"You said you wanted to destroy the fishbowl. To not leave the door open."

"Yes."

"Then it's done," she said. "You're no longer the prisoner. Or the guard. Or the architect. You're just the man who saw the illusion, and chose to leave it shattered."

A long pause.

"And if all you carry," she said, "is that you're alone, and you still choose to go forward, then

Søren… you are free. Not because the world is safe.
But because you no longer need it to be."
She let the silence linger.
"And the dream," she whispered, "is no longer a
dream. It's an opening."
And Søren, tired, unburdened, unnamed, sat in the
quiet.
The phrase still humming in his chest: *Happiness in
the Rain.*

Driving back from Dr. Jacob's office,
just beyond the edges of suburban Boston,
past open farms and slow hills stitched with green,
Søren let the conversation drift in his mind like
weather.
He reviewed the session with Sara,
her questions about meaning,
his answers, half formed, half confessed.
And then, suddenly,
he remembered something he forgot to tell her.
Something small.
But to him, it felt important.

In the dream, *the one with the pool,*

when the woman entered the water,

he caught her scent: *sandalwood and cedar.*

And in that moment,

he remembered, she had always smelled like that.

In every dream.

He just hadn't noticed until now.

He smiled faintly.

This drive, he thought, was a good time for

remembering.

Driving, for Søren, was a kind of meditation.

He called it *Drive-Thru Meditation.*

The road moved.

He stayed still.

And while the trees passed and the clouds leaned

over long meadows,

he returned to the conversation about meaning.

His search for it hadn't been particularly successful.

But then he thought:

Is there such a thing as success in the search for

meaning?

Or maybe... *the search itself is the meaning.*

It reminded him of something from meditation

practice:

Meditation isn't about going somewhere and never
coming back.
It's not a destination.
It's the repeated, humble act of returning.
Bringing the mind back.
From wherever it's wandered,
from anxiety, from narrative, from ego,
back into presence.
Not to silence the mind,
but to move it from the *driver's seat*
to the *passenger seat.*
It's not about staying there.
It's about remembering to return.
Otherwise, he thought,
even a synthetic drug can take you there,
and never bring you back.
And perhaps,
searching for meaning is just like that.
He once defined the meaning of life,
as reaching the full range of your capacity,
physical, intellectual, spiritual.
But now, that felt too clean.
Too simple.

He began to wonder if *meaning* itself

was a Western obsession.

Abraham, the prophet his mother had admired, was,

in a sense, the original architect of this doctrine.

That everything must connect.

That a soul must find its mirror.

That suffering is tolerable,

if it has meaning.

Even if it can't answer Job's grief,

it can at least justify the fire.

Søren found himself leaning toward that view,

that meaning must come from *connection.*

If there is a God, an Abrahamic one, that's ideal.

If not, then at least there must be some inner link

to the *soul of the universe.*

For years, he had wandered inside a triangle:

- The *problem of meaning*, a Western thought,

- The *problem of suffering*, a Buddhist insight,

- The *necessity of harmony*, a Taoist intuition.

He knew the three could live under one roof.

But for some reason,

he could never fully let go of the first.

He needed meaning.

He always had.

And just as the road curved toward the city again,

he remembered,

today was the last day to vacate his office at the

university.

He exhaled.

Changed the route.

And then, on impulse,

he pulled off the main road.

There was an old used bookstore near the edge of

town.

He'd passed it a dozen times,

never stopped.

Today, he did.

Just in case, he thought,

I never come this way again.

After the used bookstore, he made a U-turn and
drove back toward his office.

When he arrived, he carried two boxes, one small,
the other large.
The small one was for what he would take.
The large, for what he would discard, or more
precisely, recycle.
He unlocked the door and paused.
"Will I miss this place?" he asked himself.
Then answered,
"No.
Because it never really belonged to me."
He put on his headphones, set the music to repeat, a
Passacaglia, and began.
Lecture notes, old papers, postcards,
a stack of empty coffee cups, each with dried coffee
at the bottom,
all thrown into the recycling box.
He kept the postcard from Elena, the one she sent
when he got tenure.
And one coffee mug that read: *You Suck (but in a
good way)*.
He came to his Ph.D. diploma from *Georgetown*,
framed and hung on the wall.
"Probably the frame is worth more than the
degree," he thought.

But he didn't toss it.

He kept it, for his father.

He stacked all his books outside the door,

left a note: *Free, take whatever speaks to you.*

Only one book stayed with him:

Leibniz's Metaphysical Treatise.

An old edition, second-hand,

filled with marginalia from a reader who clearly

understood every line.

Printed in 1930.

He'd found it years ago in a used bookstore in

Zurich.

He was lost in this quiet task when he felt someone

at the door.

He pulled off his headphones.

It was Sonya and Jadip.

Both had taken his *Philosophy of Mathematics*

seminar,

the one where he always said:

"Don't chase information.

Chase skill."

And the three skills he emphasized were always the

same:

- Problem solving,

- Critical thinking,

- And storytelling.

They greeted him.

He nodded back.

"You need something?" he asked.

Sonya said:

"Professor, are you leaving?"

He replied:

"Didn't I ask you not to call me that?"

She corrected herself:

"Søren, are you leaving?"

"Yes," he said.

"Today's my last day."

Jadip hesitated, then asked:

"But why, Professor… I mean, Søren?"

He gestured to the two chairs in the room that weren't covered in papers.

"Alright, sit. Why are you here?"

Sonya answered:

"We're applying to master's programs. We wanted to ask if you could write us recommendation letters."

He paused.

"I don't hold a position anymore. Not sure if that helps or hurts your chances...

Where are you applying?"

Sonya said:

"Theoretical mathematics."

Jadip grinned:

"Computer science."

Søren nodded.

"Alright. I'll write them."

He took one of his old business cards, crossed out the university email, and wrote down his personal address.

"Email me," he said.

"Send your résumé, courses you took with me, what your projects were, and your grades."

They thanked him and got up to leave.

"Wait," Søren said.

He turned to Jadip.

"You'll be great in computer science. I think your mom will be proud."

Then to Sonya:

"But you, don't waste your time on math."

"Why not?" Sonya asked.

"Because you have a beautiful mind.

Jadip, you do too, but you were made to build.

Sonya, you were made to undo.

To dismantle foolish assumptions."

Sonya looked confused.

"Then what should I study?"

"Philosophy," he said.

"I don't mean that dusty old metaphysical garbage,

I mean philosophy of mind.

The real kind."

He stood.

"Good luck, wherever you end up.

Don't forget the email.

Remind me about the recommendation letters.

Goodbye."

Sonya didn't say a word.

There was a tightness in her throat she couldn't

untie.

She stands beside him.

The line stretches forward, but she doesn't watch it.

She watches him.

He hasn't recognized her yet.

That's all right.

He will.

She listens to the music too, not through headphones, but through the way it changes the air around them.

The boy behind them nods in rhythm.

The melody spins soft, unfinished, circling inward.

It's not the music that matters.

It's what it touches.

She feels it in him, the ache behind his posture, the quiet tilt of his head when the sound brushes memory.

He speaks.

"I'll find that music one day…"

The sentence is small, but full of *wanting*.

Jade turns slightly.

Without looking at the man, she speaks inwardly, from the heart:

"Everyone is a note in some great music.

I am an ♪F, and this man: a ♪C.

Between us humans, there are resonances, echoes of

music."

She murmurs to herself:

"*Jade, life is short,*

Find that melody."

Jade knows.

He has heard her voice.

Even if the melody hasn't finished playing yet.

She wakes up.

The rain had just stopped in Paris. A hush followed
it, like a held breath after an exhale. Jade sat across
from Luc in his quiet office, surrounded by books,
shadows and the faintest trace of drying sky.

She had shared her last dream.

She stood beside him in a line. She didn't know
why they were waiting. Or for what. But the dream
didn't require understanding. Only presence.

He hadn't recognized her. Not yet. But she knew he
would.

Luc let the silence hang, the way a conductor holds a pause before a final movement.

"You weren't standing in line for something," he said softly. "You were standing in line… for someone."

Jade didn't smile. But something in her chest stirred, like music she hadn't heard in a long time.

"I wasn't sad he didn't know me," she said. "I was waiting. I was sure he would."

Luc nodded. "That's not hope. That's knowing."

She met his gaze. "And then the music began."

"Not in your ears."

"No," she said. "Through the air. Through him. The boy behind us had headphones, but I could feel the melody. Circular. Soft. Incomplete. I watched him lean back slightly, trying to catch more of it. That small movement… I felt it."

Luc leaned forward slightly, never pushing. "What did you feel in your body?"

"Closeness," she said. "A bond. Like we were already touching something together. Even before he saw me. Even before I spoke."

He waited.

"It felt good," she added quietly. "I haven't had that feeling in a long time. Even a small brush of connection, accidental, involuntary, it felt like a thread tying me back into something real."

Luc's voice softened. "Was the joy because he recognized you… Or because you recognized yourself in his presence?"

She paused. Her voice dropped. "The second one. I've been alone a long time. Not just physically. I've lived with silence, but without a witness. It's like what someone said: *Loneliness is fine, but someone must tell you that loneliness is fine.*"

Luc tilted his head slightly. "You weren't asking him to break your silence. You just needed someone who could hear it."

She nodded.

"And when he spoke," Luc continued, "When he said, 'I'll find that music one day', did you feel like he was talking to the room? Or to you?"

"To the space between us," Jade said. "Like the words fell right where we were both standing."

"And your response, 'Find the music. Life is short,'"

"I think I was talking to myself," she said. "But also, to him. I think… I hoped he heard my heart."

Luc leaned back, not out of distance, but to hold space.

"You've carried him through many dreams. But this one was different. Not rescue. Not descent. Not silence. Just… harmony."

She nodded. "The pattern changed."

"And what does that suggest to you?"

"That it might be the end."

"Of the dreams?"

"Maybe," she said. "And I'm okay with that."

Luc gave the pause the room deserved.

"You said you don't believe in soulmates."

"I don't," she replied. "But I believe in harmony. And there are souls, very few, that can hear you before you speak. That can hold your shape without shrinking theirs."

"And if the dreams stop?"

She took a breath. "I think I'll still recognize him if I see him. There are signs. Keys. The way silence bends when he's nearby. His presence. And… his obsession with numbers."

Luc smiled. "And what will you say, if that day comes?"

Jade looked out the window, where the rain had become mist.

"I won't need to say anything," she whispered. "I'll know if he hears it."

Jade had never made a list.

No perfect man.

No perfect moment.

No imagined proposal beneath Paris rain.

She had heard those stories.

Listened politely.

Laughed when it was called for.

But she had always known that love, true love, didn't arrive as fantasy.

It arrived like breath.

Quiet.

Unasked for.

Like a vital pulse,

Beneath her skin.

She had loved before.

Deeply.

But quietly.

Never all at once.

And never for show.

Not the kind you write poems about.

The kind you *remember in silence,*

years later,

when you hear a certain kind of music

or smell coffee at the wrong time of day.

There had been a man once,

a colleague.

Sharp, generous, thoughtful in the way that drew

people in.

She had watched him fall in love with someone

else.

And she had let him.

Not out of self-denial.

But because love, to her, was not a transaction.

It didn't need to be returned to be real.

Some feelings were too clean,

to be pushed into motion.

She held that one
like a folded note she never gave away.

There were others.
Passengers on long-haul flights.
An old friend from training.
A stranger who made her laugh once in a market in
Beijing.
Each stayed,
not as stories,
but as *small lives she carried without needing to
live them.*
She had space.
Not emptiness.
But a quiet cosmos within.

She didn't fear being alone.
She feared being misunderstood.
People saw her stillness
and mistook it for completion.
But she was not done.
She was not closed.

She was open in a way few could recognize,

held wide by experience,

but unwilling to perform.

She had always believed love was real.

Not because she felt it often,

but because she never faked it.

She believed in the kind that doesn't ask for

anything.

The kind that doesn't need to name itself to survive.

She didn't believe in soulmates.

But she believed in *soul meeting soul*

across time,

across silence,

across lives.

If someone ever met her fully,

they wouldn't have to ask for her love.

They'd only have to see her

as she already was.

And she would know.

Not because he arrived with words.

But because he would carry

the same kind of silence

she had been holding all along.

Jade left Dr. Armand's office quietly.

It wasn't until she was halfway home on the Métro,

leaning against the cold glass of the carriage,

she noticed something strange.

She had just spent two weeks in Vietnam

with a man and hadn't mentioned him once.

Not to Luc.

Not even in passing.

She used to call him her *international lover*.

They had met a few times on long-haul flights,

coincidence disguised as fate.

He was handsome.

Generous.

Romantic.

Mature.

Established.

Everything a well-meaning, secretly naïve woman

is taught to want.

It didn't end badly.

Because it never really began.

She wasn't heartbroken.

She hadn't counted on it.

And yet,

she had just paid 250 euros

and crossed Paris

to talk about *a man in a dream.*

So, what was wrong with the international lover?

Nothing.

And that was exactly the problem.

There was no pause in him.

No hesitation.

No trace of the quiet question mark she always

looked for in someone's eyes.

That thin silence,

the one that lives between two silences.

The one that says: *"I've seen something. I don't*

know what it means yet."

He was too happy.

And she kept wondering,

why?

It wasn't that he was empty.

She was too, in her own way.

But what unsettled her,

what made her feel suddenly *far* from him,

was that *he didn't seem to mind.*

Søren no longer believed in boundaries,

at least not outside mathematics.

In equations, boundaries were sacred.

They defined domains, thresholds, limits.

A function respected its boundary,

just as a wave respects the shore:

not because it must be crossed,

but because it completes the form.

But out here,

In the world of breath and silence,

such clarity unraveled.

People spoke of life and death,

of sleep and wakefulness,

as if they were separate states.

But Søren knew better.

Transitions were messy.

Edges, blurred.

Departures, unmarked.

Sleep didn't end when eyes opened,

and waking wasn't a return.

And this, more than he ever admitted,

disturbed him deeply.

He stood by the window of his apartment.

Evening light cast long shadows across the floor.

Behind him, the kettle began to whistle.

But he didn't move.

His mind was elsewhere,

turning, circling.

He had seen that house in his dream again.

This time, the hallway was longer.

Windows opened inward.

He passed rooms that were unfamiliar,

but somehow,

somehow the house remembered him.

A dizzying staircase. Grooved wooden railings.

This time, he was descending from the second floor.

He didn't know why he was there,

Or how he'd arrived on the second floor.

There were many rooms.

Each had a number,

But someone had scratched them out.

For the first time,

he couldn't read the numbers.

Then the dream shifted.

Now he was outside the house.

It had a sloped roof,

old red bricks,

ivy climbing around the windows and the front

door.

A lantern hung beside the door,

Its flame teased by the breeze.

A curtain swayed in the upstairs window.

Later, he rose and turned off the kettle.

Poured the water.

But he didn't drink.

He only sat.

There had been an order to the dream.

It wasn't memory.

It wasn't imagination.

The thought stayed with him

until he opened a book he'd picked up

at a used bookstore a week earlier.

A registry of old estates and rural houses,

their histories inked in brown,

their photos faded soft.

He flipped through it slowly.

Page 233.

A house on the edge of a forest in Portugal.

More precisely, on the outskirts of Lisbon.

Once a family estate,

now a private guesthouse.

The name meant nothing to him.

The family history even less.

But the image,

that sloped roof.

The three windows on the upper floor.

The gravel path curving to the door

exactly the same way.

Almost identical to the house in his dream.

He stared at the page for a long time.

There was no rational path from this discovery to

what he'd do next.

He stayed frozen on page 233.

233, a Fibonacci number.

This time, the dream had brought no number.

Wakefulness had.

And the house, *Domus Animae,*

had a shape that nothing else did.

He made his decision.

Lisbon had called him.

That midnight, without ceremony,

he called the guesthouse.

It was 7 a.m. there.

A young woman answered, her English fluent:

"From April 27 to May 2.

Room number 21.

Yes, your room is confirmed.

We look forward to seeing you, Dr. Hossein."

After the call ended,

Søren had even more questions.

The girl had asked for nothing except the dates.

No credit card.

No phone number or address.

Not even his name.

And yet, she knew it.

Not just knew it, she recognized him.

And most strange of all:

"Since when do they assign a room number during booking?"

Twenty-one. Another Fibonacci number.

He no longer knew where, in the landscape of sleep and waking, he stood.

"The house remembers me."

The numbers have crossed over from dream to day.

And the woman?

The woman.

The final unknown in the equation of his dreams.

This was no longer the boundary between sleep and
waking.

It was the boundary between madness and the
reclamation of his soul.

A room had been reserved.

Five nights.

One guest.

No company.

No expectations.

Only a sense,

that something waited for him

on the other side.

The next morning, Søren booked a flight to Lisbon.

A direct flight,

expensive and irrational,

especially for a professor who had just left his job,

and was heading on a journey he couldn't quite

explain.

But he felt it:

he was on a path where he would either lose his

mind,

or retrieve his soul.

So instead,

he chose a cheaper route:

with a layover in Toronto.

He didn't mind.

He wasn't staying.

Toronto had nothing to say to him.

A city without soul.

Efficient, polished, emotionless.

But he wasn't seeking soul in a transit lounge.

It was just a station.

A short pause.

Nothing more.

He packed late, as always.

Didn't take much.

- His laptop.

- A dark brown coat, his usual companion for
  uncertain weather.

- And two books. Printed, not digital.
  Because printed books had a soul.
  The soul of paper books was in the pauses,
  the notes he had scribbled in the margins,
  The tears that had once fallen on certain pages.

And how each rereading turned them into
something else.
These two books were the ones he turned to
when nothing else worked:
- *Gitanjali* by *Rabindranath Tagore*
- *Report to Greco* by *Nikos Kazantzakis*
He didn't know how many times he had read them.
Ten? Probably fewer.
But that wasn't the point.
The point was this:
When you leave on a journey whose meaning you
don't yet understand,
you carry voices with you,
voices that, at least once,
had left you a little less hopeless.
Everything was simple.
There was nothing left to organize.
He had been ready.
As always.

Søren was sitting alone at the edge of a crowded
gate in Toronto Pearson airport. He hadn't slept

much. He rarely did on travel days. The terminal
hummed with motion and quiet noise, luggage
wheels, muted announcements, disposable coffee
cups, voices from nowhere.

He watched people move across the concourse and
imagined looking at them through the lens of a
camera.

No sound.

Just motion.

People coming. People going. Some with a purpose.
Some stalling for time.

Some searched for their gates.

Others lingered at smoking booths, stared at
departure boards and browsed shops they didn't
need.

No one knew where they were headed. Not really.
From the outside, there was no way to tell who was
on their way to a honeymoon, a funeral, a business
deal, or a final visit. Every face concealed a
timeline. Every movement carried a reason.

And yet,

there was one certainty.

*In a few hours, maybe a day or two, none of them
will still be here.*

They would vanish. Quietly. In sequence. One
departure at a time.

They would take their belongings, their destinations
and their unsaid thoughts.

The airport would remain.

The seats, the shops, the glowing signs.

The cigarette booths and coffee kiosks.

Even the air would feel the same.

Nothing would register the change.

Even friendships forged in those brief hours would
fade the moment flights were called.

People parted, and the camera panned away.

Søren sat with that thought for a long while.

He loved soccer. One of the few things he had in
common with the ordinary man.

Once, he had watched grainy footage of an Old
World Cup final, Brazil, perhaps, in the 1930s.

Maracanã Stadium. He had murmured to himself as
he watched:

Over a hundred thousand people saw this match in
person.

Then he had paused.

There wasn't even the tiniest chance that any of
them were still alive.

Probability humbles us.

All of them, every spectator, was gone.

Ashes.

Names forgotten.

And yet,

Maracanã still stood.

The grass was mowed.

The lights, replaced.

The seats filled again and again with new arrivals.

Life is an airport.

We arrive.

We wait.

We depart.

The lens might be wide, but it will always lose us
eventually.

We take nothing from it.

And what we leave behind, if anything, will be
absorbed without ceremony.

The world remains.

The gates rotate.

The seats are refilled.

And the next wave begins.

25 An Accident in Form, Destiny in Essence

When she got home,

her next flight was already scheduled:

Direct to *Detroit.*

She didn't feel anything in particular about the

destination.

No attachment.

No excitement.

But something quiet and persistent, was telling her:

this journey would be different.

Pilots often carry a quiet thought before takeoff:

Maybe this is my last flight.

But this wasn't that kind of feeling.

She wasn't afraid of death.

It was something else,

like a shift waiting beneath the surface.

A slow-turning hinge inside the psyche.

And Jade had a good psyche.

Clear.

Attentive.

Not dramatic, just listening.

She started packing earlier than usual:

- Her airline uniform: clean, ironed.
- A small kit of makeup, though she rarely used much.
- A few changes of clothes.
- A large greenish scarf, soft and square.
- A book: *Fate Is the Hunter. Ernest Gann's* memoir of skies, solitude, and near misses.
- And one small bottle of perfume, a 100ml gift, from the international lover. On the label, in faded serif letters, it read:
  The scent of Sandalwood and Cedar.

That was it.

She stood by the suitcase for a moment.

Looked once around the room.

She didn't speak.

She was ready.

On the long return flight from Detroit to Paris,

AF 377,

somewhere above the Atlantic Ocean, a serious technical failure occurred.

Serious.

One of those failures that isn't catastrophic, but could become so.

They diverted.

Lisbon was the closest.

The landing was smooth. The ground crew calm.

"It'll need at least forty-eight hours," they told her. "Bad luck."

The crew was sent to a hotel near the airport.

Standard protocol.

Showers. Sleep. Wait for clearance.

But Jade had a friend, Paulo, who lived just outside Lisbon, in the northern hills.

She rented a car.

Planned to surprise him.

Even though she was tired enough to fall asleep at the wheel.

She didn't tell anyone she was going.

An hour into the drive, the engine stuttered.

Then failed.

No crash. No drama.

Just silence and smoke, and a dashboard blinking in defeat.

She coasted to the side of the road.

A narrow stretch of highway framed by stone walls

and olive trees.

No signal.

No service.

The sun was already dropping behind the hills.

She left the car.

Started walking.

Her shoes weren't made for this kind of road, and

the suitcase handle kept twisting.

She considered turning back.

But something tugged,

not forward exactly,

just *away*.

Through a crooked path between trees and dry-

stone walls, she saw it.

At first, it looked like a house.

No sign. No lights in the upper windows.

Only a small lantern near the door.

And carved into the wood, almost hidden beneath a

layer of age and ivy:

Domus Animae.

She didn't know Latin.

But something in her chest answered it anyway.

Not curiosity.

Not logic.

Just a quiet recognition.

She stepped forward.

The door opened before she could knock again.

A woman stood there, older, with silver hair pulled into a braid.

Not unfriendly. Not exactly warm.

But *steady*.

She said nothing at first. Just studied Jade for a moment.

Then:

"Room thirteen."

Jade blinked.

"I didn't make a reservation."

The woman nodded once.

"You didn't have to."

She handed her a key. Brass, heavy. A number etched into its oval tag: *13*

No forms. No ID. No card.

No explanations.

Jade opened her mouth to speak,

but realized there was nothing to ask.

She followed the woman down a hallway lit by soft

amber sconces.

The walls weren't decorated; they were

remembered.

Not staged, not styled. Just… worn in the way old

houses are when they've been lived in properly.

When they reached the room, the woman paused

and looked at her again.

"You'll sleep well here," she said.

Jade nodded.

She hadn't meant to say anything.

But before the door closed, the words left her mouth

anyway:

"What does it mean? The name? *Domus Animae*?"

The woman smiled gently.

"It means the house of the soul."

"But most people just feel it. You don't need to

translate it."

And then she was gone.

Jade stepped into the room.

Put down her bag.

Removed her shoes.

She didn't check her phone.

She sat on the edge of the bed.

Listened to the silence.

And for the first time in years,

she didn't feel like she had to be anywhere else.

The forest came into view gradually, first as a

smear of green,

Then, as a curtain drawing itself across the road.

Søren eased his foot off the accelerator

and let the silence of the trees swallow the hum of

the engine.

The GPS had gone silent ten minutes ago.

He hadn't minded.

It felt appropriate.

The inn did not appear all at once.

It emerged, piece by piece, through gaps in the

branches,

a sloped roof,

a corner of old brick,

a flicker of a curtain in an upstairs window.

And then, the full view:

A modest but elegant manor at the edge of a

clearing,

It's form, unsettling in its familiarity.

Søren had seen it before.

In dreams.

In memory.

Or perhaps in the photograph on page 233.

He pulled the car to a stop along the gravel path.

No one else was arriving.

No one was leaving.

The inn felt suspended,

as if waiting for its cue.

He stepped out.

Retrieved his small black bag from the trunk.

The air was cool.

Before he could knock, the door opened.

A woman stood there.

Dark hair pinned back.

Clothing simple but neat.

She smiled, not as a greeting, but as if she

recognized him.

"Mr. Hussain?"

He nodded.

"Your room is ready.

Dinner is served from seven to nine.

Breakfast until ten."

She handed him a brass key on a worn leather tag.

"Room twenty-one. Up the left stairwell."

The check-in required nothing more.

No form.

No signature.

Just a glance, a nod,

and the key passed from one hand to another.

He walked slowly up the stairs,

inhaling the scent of wood and old linen.

The numbers on the doors made no obvious sense.

20 was missing.

27 came before 24.

When he reached 21, he paused,

touched the tag again,

then unlocked the door.

The room was perfectly still.

A narrow bed.

A writing desk.

A chair.

A window facing the woods.

Everything was in its place.

Søren sat on the bed and let the quiet settle around
him.

He did not unpack.

He did not lie down.

He simply looked.

The air felt charged,

not ominous,

not inviting.

Just aware.

He knew, without knowing how,

that the inn was already calculating him.

Not judging.

Just observing.

As if the building itself was waiting

to see how he would fill the variables it offered.

And when he finally lay back

and closed his eyes,

it did not feel like sleep.

It felt like insertion.

On his first morning at the inn, Søren stayed in his
room longer than he expected.
He didn't rush for breakfast.

Didn't glance at the schedule pinned to the wall.

Instead, he began to observe, the space that had

been assigned to him:

the furniture, the corners, and the light coming

through a window he hadn't noticed the night

before.

The room was tidy. Clean. Quiet.

And completely unattached to him.

This world,

with its neon cities, glass towers, prestige jobs,

flawless weddings, curated social feeds, and

unreachable wealth,

was nothing more than an inn.

Beautiful.

Alluring.

But an inn, nonetheless.

Even the grandest suite is just a temporary

arrangement.

And most of us aren't even in that suite.

We peer in from the hallway, imagining, envying.

That top one-tenth of one percent lives as if gravity

itself does not apply to them.

The rest of us?

We watch.

We dream.

We mimic.

But beneath it all, Søren thought, this world is a
hotel room.

We enjoy the view.

But we don't own the view.

We are only passing through.

Look a little closer, and the shine of the hotel room
begins to fade.

Lift the edge of the bedspread, and there's the dust.

Pull back the curtain of this world, and suffering
reveals itself,

Lives sacrificed, voices silenced, souls torn apart in
the most merciless ways.

The illusion of fullness.

Just like life.

We fill our homes and days with objects and
positions,

books we've never read, clothes we never wear,

titles we never asked for,

and we call it wealth, status, prestige.

Søren looked around the room again.

Everything had been perfectly prepared for
someone like him.

And yet, none of it was his.

Not even his reflection in the mirror.

The hallway on the second floor turned sharply, as if unsure of its own direction. Søren followed it anyway. The light here was different, not darker, just denser. A hallway that seemed to think before continuing.

Room 19, then 23. All odd numbers. Room 25 had no knob. Room 27 had no door at all.

And then,

a door with no number. No plaque. No frame where a plaque might have once been.

Just the surface of a door, perfectly still, without history.

A *dummy room*, he thought.

A variable in the structure that might never receive a value.

A ghost placeholder in the equation.

He paused in front of it, longer than he intended.

Something about it unsettled him, not emotionally, but structurally. Conceptually.

It reminded him of a paradox in cosmology: a physicist deserved the Nobel for showing that certain measurements in the universe could *never* be completed.

Not because of technological limitations, but because the universe wouldn't last long enough to finish the act of measuring.

He remembered the phrasing:

If a quantity cannot be measured before the collapse of reality, does it ever truly exist as a quantity?

The door seemed to whisper that same question.

Was this room part of the inn if no one would ever enter it?

He pressed his hand against it. Cool wood. No sound behind it.

And then the deeper discomfort came:

We divide the world, unquestioningly, into *quantity* and *quality*.

As if the measurable were separate from the meaningful.

As if matter could be divorced from essence.

Plato had done this. And we still lived inside his shadow.

But what if it was never true?

What if *meaning itself was measurable, and matter was always meaningful*, but only from the inside?

What if the border between quantity and quality was just another frame we mistook for a wall?

And what if all our metaphysics were built not on truth, but on the need to *divide*?

He stepped back from the door.

The real world isn't built on boundaries.

It's built on assumptions.

She hadn't planned to think.

Not this morning.

Not after a night of strange dreams and half-sleep.

Not with the birds already echoing through the

trees,

and the light pouring sideways through the linen

curtain.

But the stillness of the room wouldn't let her leave

it yet.

She sat on the edge of the bed,

wrapped in the robe the inn had left at the door.

She had clarity.

Not all the time,

but more than most.

Flying had taught her that.

That control and surrender weren't opposites.

That the way forward was rarely felt at the

beginning of a journey,

but only in the small adjustments made along the

way.

She had learned how to make decisions in silence.

To hold course through uncertainty.

To land even when the runway wasn't visible.

But no one had ever asked her where she learned to carry herself

so quietly.

No one ever asked what it cost her to make it look effortless.

It wasn't loneliness that haunted her.

It was invisibility.

People admired her calm.

Her composure.

Her timing.

But they didn't really see her.

Not the parts that mattered.

They saw professionalism.

Not presence.

Strength.

Not stillness.

She had dreams too.

She just didn't talk about them.

Not because she didn't believe in them,

but because when she shared them,

they turned into someone else's story.

She preferred to carry them alone.

Like small instruments.

Tools no one else knew how to hold.

There was always a house.

There was often a man.

There was sometimes a child she couldn't name.

But always,

always,

there was that strange silence.

Not emptiness.

Not absence.

Just... *waiting*.

She hadn't been looking for meaning.

She had long since stopped trying to name it.

What she was looking for,

if she could even say it,

was a kind of recognition.

Someone who could see her,

not for what she carried well,

but for what she never let fall.

Someone who didn't mistake her stillness for being
done.
She stood.
Crossed the room to the window.
Pushed it open.
The wind moved through the trees with a sound she
recognized,
though she couldn't place it.
She breathed it in slowly.
It smelled like morning.
Like wood, memory and breath.
She didn't need to understand it.
She only needed to stay long enough
for it to speak back.

The journey had already begun, speaking to him.

Not loudly.

Not with words.

But with signs.

Little ones at first, a flicker in his chest, a shift in the wind, the way the light slanted across the dashboard as if guiding him somewhere.

On his first full day, Søren decided to drive into Lisbon's city center.

He took the rental car, set the GPS, and merged into traffic,

Only to find himself trapped.

At first, it seemed like a typical traffic jam.

Construction maybe.

A political march.

Something temporary.

But after twenty minutes, he realized:

This wasn't a simple jam.

The streets weren't just clogged.

They were frozen.

Locked in place like the moment before an earthquake, tense with silence.

It started, as collapses often do, with something small:

A power outage.

First, the electricity disappeared.

Then the traffic lights blinked off.

Then the cell towers sighed and died.

No signal.

No internet.

No phones.

No voice to scream into the void.

The credit card machines stopped working.

The shops locked their doors.

ATMs went dark.

The collapse rippled outward like an infection.

France to Portugal.

Chain after chain snapped.

In just a few hours, western civilization showed its true fragility:

No nukes, no pandemics necessary.

Just one tiny break in the circuit.

A whisper in the wires, and everything fell.

Søren stood on the sidewalk, hands in his pockets, watching.

Not happy.

Not surprised.

The outer world was crumbling,

brick by brick,

in rhythm with something inside him.

He had a name for it:

Technological Overreliance.

We built tools to make life easier.

And in doing so,

without noticing,

we built prisons for ourselves.

Comfortable, elegant prisons, lined with glass and
steel, disguised as progress.

He thought of the patio door in his old apartment.

How the lock never worked unless you unlocked it
first.

A ridiculous little trick of design.

You had to move backward to move forward.

And now Lisbon,

in the half-light of a dead grid,

was playing the same game.

The lock had clicked.

The city was sealed.

No way in. No way out. Just stillness, and the sound

of questions he hadn't yet formed.

Søren wasn't against modern life.

He was against *depending* on it.

A three-year-old sobbed because his mother's

iPhone had died.

A young Italian woman, stranded, cried because she

couldn't return to Rome for her birthday.

No trains.

No planes.

No cash in her pockets.

Her voice rose above the silence like a bird trapped

in glass.

Somewhere on a street corner,

a homeless man holding a cup full of coins

was suddenly richer than all of them.

And Søren noticed, with quiet amusement,

that the young Italian woman's anger wasn't just at

the situation.

It was directed at her boyfriend,

for not doing enough

to fix the world.

She needed someone to blame. He, unfortunately,

was available.

When the *physical grid* broke,

the *emotional grid* cracked, too.

Love, like electricity, was failing under pressure.

But Søren wasn't here to lecture anyone about

modernity.

Not today.

He was here for something else.

For a conversation that was still unnamed.

For an answer he wasn't sure how to phrase.

Lisbon, beautiful and breathing,

lay on life support for half a day.

And somewhere inside that broken city,

Søren knew:

The real journey had just begun.

It wasn't in the map. It wasn't in the signal.

It was in the silence,

and what rose up to meet him inside it.

The first night at the inn passed strangely for Jade. Trapped by a sudden collapse of the local power grid, she could do nothing but wait.

She spent the long, slow day walking the grounds. She was circling the silent building, its pale walls washed by the uncertain light of a powerless afternoon. The inn itself seemed suspended in a kind of waking sleep, neither welcoming nor hostile, simply... paused.

Even the breeze through the trees seemed quieter, as if the absence of electricity had drained the sound from the air. It was a stillness that made her feel both calmed and unmoored, like a dream she couldn't wake from.

Without electricity, without connection, the usual rhythms of travel dissolved.

She realized, with a quiet sigh, that even if the power returned soon, the maintenance crews at the airport would likely face longer delays. Flights would be pushed, rescheduled, and lost into the heavy machinery of disrupted time.

The invisible infrastructure that made the world run, timing, schedules, access, had collapsed. She was suspended in a kind of limbo, a forgotten corner of someone else's plan.

Night fell softly.

At last, the lights flickered back to life.

The world blinked awake again, humming with fragile, renewed current.

Jade wasted no time. She called the rental agency first, arranging for a tow truck to retrieve her car, still ditched along the narrow suburban road.

Then, heart slightly lifted, she called Paulo, the one familiar voice she trusted in Lisbon.

No answer at first.

But minutes later, the call returned.

Paulo, warm and apologetic, explained the blackouts had thrown the whole city into confusion.

He offered to pick her up himself the next morning.

"Come, Jade," he said, his voice carrying a smile.

"We'll have lunch. I'll show you the real Lisbon. Not the tourist postcards. The bones, the breath, the soul of the city."

Jade agreed.

And without quite knowing why, she felt a quiet thread of hope weave itself through her exhaustion. It was a small thing, an offer, a plan, but in the haze of disconnection, it felt like being pulled back toward the world.

The next morning, Paulo was on time.

"Hi Paulo, good to see you," Jade said warmly as he pulled her into a light embrace. "Actually, two nights ago I wanted to surprise you... But I got surprised by that stupid car."

Paulo laughs warmly, the sound light and easy against the soft morning air as they walk along a sunlit Lisbon street.

The city around them stirred with life, vendors setting up carts, shutters creaking open, distant music spilling from a window. It felt like the day itself was exhaling.

"Ah, Jade! That sounds exactly like Lisbon. She loves to surprise, even when she's not trying."

Paulo adjusted his sunglasses, glancing sideways at her, full of affection but no judgment.

"And I am the one who is happy. Look, here you are, alive, safe, and now in the best company."

He gestured ahead, where the streets slope gently toward a broad plaza. The stone beneath their feet glowed pale gold.

"Let me properly welcome you. First, we visit *Praça do Comércio*, the old royal gateway. After the great earthquake of 1755, they rebuilt this whole square. Stronger, grander. Lisbon rose again from the dust."

He paused, letting her see the sweeping arc of colonnades, the towering archway that frames the sky.

"You see. Lisbon never stays broken for long. Even when the whole world thinks she should."

He smiled, but his voice carries a soft undercurrent, as if he was not speaking only about cities.

They walked a few steps in comfortable silence before he continued, his voice growing more thoughtful.

"You know, Jade... I believe every city has a soul. Not just old stones and new streets. A real soul. Some are proud. Some are wounded.

Lisbon... she is tender. She hides her wounds in music and sunlight."

He looked at her again, more quietly now.

"And maybe people are like that, too."

"What do you mean by Lisbon having a soul?" she asked. "You talk about cities like they are living entities. Do you think Paris has a soul, too? Teach me by contradiction. Do you know any city that does not have a soul? Dubai?" Paulo chuckled, but not dismissively. His hand lifted briefly as if balancing an invisible scale.

"Ah, Jade, you understand better than you think." He slowed his steps a little, letting the rhythm of the walk match the rhythm of his thoughts.

"Yes. Some cities live. Some cities... merely function."

He gestured toward the broad river ahead, the Tagus, shimmering faintly under the pale Lisbon sun.

"Lisbon has soul because she has *memory*. You feel it, not just in the buildings, but in the way light falls against cracked walls, the way a song rises from a window, the way sorrow and celebration sit side by side at a table. She remembers loss, earthquakes, dictatorships, departures, and still sings."

He turned slightly toward her, eyes earnest.

"Paris, yes, she has a soul too. But a different one. Proud, layered, perfumed with centuries of ambition. Paris loves the gaze of the world. Lisbon? Lisbon doesn't care if you look. She stays beautiful anyway."

He smiled faintly.

"And Dubai? No, Dubai has no soul. Dubai is a machine. Efficient. Dazzling. But nothing has rooted there yet. No grief, no collective laughter, no slow, painful forgiveness. Without memory, without scars... There is no soul."

He let the words settle. A light breeze lifted a strand of Jade's hair.

"Maybe that's the real test, Jade. Does the place make you remember things you didn't know you forgot? Does it break your heart a little, just by standing still?"

He laughed gently again, trying to lighten the sudden seriousness.

"You asked for a contradiction. I say: a city without brokenness is a city without soul."

"Interesting observation, Paulo," she said thoughtfully. "Do you think when people are broken and crushed with unfulfilled wishes, lost lives, and defeated by their own bravery, they have a soul too? Is it extendable to nations and ideologies?"

Paulo walked silently for a few steps; his hands tucked loosely into his jacket pockets. The morning crowds moved around them, tourists, students, old men with folded newspapers, but it felt as if they were moving through a thinner, more private layer of the city.

"Yes," he said finally, his voice low, almost reluctant.

"I think so. Maybe... especially then."

He glanced over at Jade, searching her face, not to argue, but to share something raw.

"When a person breaks, really breaks, it's like a window shattering.

Most people rush to fix it, to erase the break.

But some... some leave the cracks.

They live with them.

They let the cracks catch the light differently."

He breathed out slowly.

"That's when a soul is born, I think.

Not from perfection.

But from carrying the beauty and the terror of being unfinished."

He pointed gently toward the tiled walls they pass, cracked azulejos, chipped but still glowing blue under the sun.

"As for nations, for ideologies... yes. They can have a soul too.

But they pay a price."

He smiled, but it was a sad, weary smile.

"Empires that forget their failures lose their soul. Movements that deny their own betrayals lose their soul."

He paused, then added softer:

"Maybe that's why some dreams survive and others don't.

Not because they win... but because they know they lost something along the way and remember it."

He stopped walking, facing her more fully now, his voice dropping to almost a whisper.

"And maybe, Jade...

Maybe that's true for people, too."

"Then I have a thick soul," she said, laughing softly. "Hahaha.

Since the last time we met, I think it was our trip to Istanbul, another city with soul, I have had so many setbacks, heartbreaking moments.

Everyone thinks I am strong. But I am not.

Some people do register my vulnerabilities."

She paused, voice thinning.

"... Then I have soul, don't I?"

Paulo listened, really listened, as if every word she spoke sketched something visible in the air between them.

When she laughed, he smiled too, but his eyes remained serious, soft.

"Ah, Jade..."

He said her name almost like a sigh, not out of pity, but with a kind of deep recognition.

"You have a soul so thick, so layered, so alive... it could carry whole cities inside it."

He reached out lightly, almost ceremonially, and tapped two fingers over his heart.

"Strength isn't the absence of brokenness.

It's the art of carrying it, like an old tapestry, full of

torn places, but still beautiful because it holds the history of your fight."

He chuckled quietly, but there was something like reverence underneath.

"You fooled them, Jade. You wore your strength so gracefully, so silently, they mistook it for being invincible."

He lifted his hand again, this time toward the broad expanse of the *Praça*, sunlight flooding the old stones.

"And yes, Istanbul... Lisbon... they understand you. Because they, too, know what it means to be wounded and still sing."

He fell into step beside her again, slower now, almost reluctant to break the moment.

"Maybe that's why you understand these places better than most.

Because your soul, thick, cracked, golden in its broken places, listens when the cities speak."

He looked at her sideways, a small, almost mischievous smile tugging at his mouth.

"And between you and me, Jade...

The ones who feel weak are often carrying the greatest light."

"I think these are compliments," she said lightly, trying to steer herself back from the edge of feeling. "Yes, I am like Lisbon, like Istanbul, or even like Athens, full of setbacks, surrenders...
But I still try not to give up."
She paused, eyes distant.
"I deal with my loneliness, but I need some kind of reaffirmation by a soul that witnesses my loneliness.
Do you get what I mean?
If nobody sees the vulnerabilities of Lisbon, that devastating earthquake, the tsunami after that, Salazar, etc., etc., I think Lisbon would cease to exist.
I feel I am at the brink of that."
Paulo stopped walking. Right there, in the middle of the old square, under the gentle Lisbon sun, among the tourists and pigeons and distant shouts of café waiters, he turned fully to her.
"I get it, Jade."
His voice was low, steady, no pity, no rush, only the slow weight of understanding that few people ever offer.
"You don't need someone to fix you.

You don't need someone to carry you.

You need someone to *see* you.”

He searched her face, and for the first time, there

was a trace of something almost broken in his own

expression.

“To witness the whole architecture of you,

the cracks,

the abandoned courtyards,

the silent rooms you locked long ago.”

He breathed in deeply, the salty breeze off the river

catching his jacket.

“Lisbon survived the earthquake because the people

remembered her.

Not because they rebuilt walls, but because they

refused to forget the wounds beneath the stones.”

He softened, his voice like a thread tying her back

to something real, something rooted.

“And you... You will survive, too.

But maybe, just maybe, you don’t have to do it

unseen.”

He let the words linger, offering her not a solution,

but a place to stand beside someone who knew what

loneliness *really* feels like.

“You said you're like Lisbon, like Athens, like

Istanbul.

And you're right.

The greatest cities... the greatest souls... don't vanish because of pain.

They vanish when no one believes their ruins still sing."

He smiled, quietly fierce.

"And your ruins, Jade, they sing."

"I think I understand what you mean. I read somewhere, I don't remember where, that pain is like gas: it spreads through the entire space. Pain fills the whole soul, but pleasure does not. That's why Lisbon has a soul, because she has felt pain in every single brick. But Dubai was built only yesterday, on victory, glory, and function."

Paulo listened closely, more than listened, he absorbed her words like someone taking in an ancient truth rediscovered after a long forgetting."

"Exactly, Jade."

He spoke slowly now, not lecturing, not explaining, just offering the natural unfolding of what she herself already knew.

"Pain expands.

It fills every invisible space.

It carves its presence into walls, into stones, into bloodlines."

He turned, gesturing gently toward the vast expanse of the old square, the sunlight bouncing off the worn stones, the history breathing through every crack.

"Lisbon has soul because it carries the memory of every crack and fall.

It carries them not as shame...

but as testimony."

His voice lowered, and the words grew almost reverent.

"And Dubai? You're right.

Dubai is a monument to victory without memory.

Glory without scar.

Function without longing."

He tilted his head slightly, smiling at her, not patronizing, but proud.

"You understand something most people never dare to face.

Pain does not just break.

It builds."

He fell into step beside her again, the pace slow, the air between them charged with something neither can name.

"Maybe that's why, when we love someone truly, or a place, or even a dream,

We don't love the perfection.

We love the way the cracks let the light out."

He laughed very softly, shaking his head as if amused by the strange, aching logic of it all.

"And you, Jade... you are a city made of light escaping through all the cracks you thought would destroy you."

Jade felt herself blink hard against the sting in her eyes.

She inhaled shakily.

"I was defeated by love, Paulo," she said. "Not once.

Recently, I have been having dreams that I cannot understand.

They are not about love, they are about something asking... or better, inviting my care."

Paulo heard the shift in her voice, that slight tremor that real confession always carried.

He slowed again, almost instinctively, as if giving her story room to breathe.

"Dreams..."

He said the word like it held weight, ancient and unfinished.

"Dreams aren't puzzles to be solved, Jade.

They are invitations.

Maps drawn in languages older than our waking minds."

He glanced at her, and his expression was different now, almost tender, almost solemn.

"You say you feel something asking for your care.

Maybe it's not something outside you.

Maybe it's something inside, a part of you long exiled,

waiting not for rescue... but for recognition."

They reached a narrow alley opening onto a small square.

He gestured toward a stone fountain in the center, cracked, lichen-covered, but still running with thin threads of water.

"Look. Even broken things can still flow."

He turned fully to her now, not smiling, not laughing, just steady.

"Maybe your dreams aren't about love in the way you once understood it.

Maybe they are about something deeper.

A call to turn your care inward.

Not to abandon the world, but to hold it differently.

Not by possession... but by presence.”

He softened, his voice falling almost to a whisper.

“And Jade,

not everyone hears that call.

Even fewer answer it.”

He let the silence stretch between them, not heavy,

not awkward,

but full, like a cup being offered with both hands.

“Maybe these dreams aren’t warning you.

Maybe they are welcoming you.”

Jade took a breath.

“What if you see an eight-year-old kid shivering

because you are asking him to go into the darkness,

although it was not you, or you see a similar kid in

real life traveling alone, and your heart wants to

stop...

These dreams and real-life experiences have

captivated me.”

She touched her chest lightly.

“I didn't believe in bliss or calling, but I might

have.”

Paulo listened in complete stillness, no
interruptions, no shifting weight, no polite smiles.
Only that rare kind of listening that feels like
shelter.

"Jade..."

He said her name slowly, as if weighing its gravity.

"What you just described,

it's not confusion.

it's awakening."

He stepped closer, his voice low but clear, steady
like a hand reaching into uncertain waters.

"If you see the child,

in dreams, in strangers, in reflections, you can't
explain.

Then you are already called."

He lifted his hand slightly, almost touching the air
between them.

"The darkness... the fear... they aren't punishments.
They are thresholds."

He held her gaze, gently but without retreat.

"You were never pushing that child into the
darkness, Jade.

You were standing there, bearing witness to his
fear, his trembling, his hesitation."

His voice roughened slightly, the emotion undeniable.

"And that alone... the willingness to stand beside the vulnerable, not to drag them, not to abandon them.

That is the beginning of real care."

He glanced away for a brief second, breathing in the ancient Lisbon air, as if borrowing strength from the stones around them.

"You said you never believed in bliss.

Maybe bliss was never the goal."

He looked back at her, almost fiercely now, but with unmistakable tenderness.

"Maybe the real calling is not to find bliss.

But to become a shelter,

for a trembling child,

for a lonely traveler,

for your own soul standing at the edge of the unknown."

He paused, letting the words settle like slow rain.

"And Jade...

Few are given that invitation.

Fewer still are brave enough to accept it."

He smiled then, the smallest smile, not of comfort,
but of deep respect.

"You are not lost.

You are being asked to *arrive*."

Jade laughed suddenly, wiping her eyes with the
sleeve of her jacket.

"Ok, let's change the conversation. It became too
serious," she said, grinning through tears.

"I am here to see you and have lunch, and have real
Portuguese food.

By the way, your car has a soul too.

It is a piece of crap."

Paulo burst out laughing, a real, full-bodied laugh
that echoed slightly off the old stone walls of the
alley.

"Ah, there she is! The Jade I missed."

He threw up his hands dramatically, playing along,
his voice full of mock offense.

"My car does have a soul, an ancient, stubborn,
grumpy soul! Like a retired sailor who refuses to
die because he still has bad songs to sing."

He grinned wide, the serious weight between them
dissolving like mist under sunlight.

"Come on, menina.

Let's get you real Portuguese food, none of that
tourist garbage.
Grilled sardines, *Caldo Verde*, and *Vinho Verde* so
cold it could resurrect your faith in life."
He swept his hand grandly toward a narrow side
street, where the smell of garlic and lemon already
wove through the air.
"And after lunch... maybe we find a café by the
river, sit under a broken umbrella, and mock my
poor, cursed car some more, yes?"
He laughed again, light, easy, infectious.
"Lisbon is stubborn.
So are you.
So am I.
It's a perfect afternoon."
He offered his arm, old-fashioned and gallant, the
way he always did when he knew Jade needed a
friend, not a philosopher.

They had left to eat grilled sardines,
but something was left unsaid.
If Søren had been there,
he surely would have said it:

People think it's the people who give cities their

soul.

But that's not true.

It's the *narratives* that give cities their soul.

People are only the words that shape those

narratives.

Narratives pile up in layers,

like a book read too many times.

Like Lisbon, where the Romans, the Carthaginians,

the Phoenicians, the Spaniards, the Celts, and the

Arabs each wrote their bitter and sweet stories over

it.

The souls of Lisbon, Istanbul, Isfahan, Baghdad,

Delhi, Athens.

It's the stories that have settled into them, page after

page.

And if there's no one left to bear witness to those

stories,

then those cities,

like Ctesiphon, like Petra,

have no longer soul.

Søren had always wondered:

Is man greater than life?

No one really knows.

But one thing is certain,

the narratives are greater than life.

On the drive back to the inn, Paulo turned on the
radio.

A young woman was singing in English, her voice
imperfect, a little raw:

"...When you hurt me, I knew I had a heart..."

But Jade heard it differently:

"...When you hurt me, I knew I had a soul..."

Paulo, as if remembering something, changed the
station.

Now, a haunting Portuguese ballad filled the car.

A deep, aching voice of a woman carrying
something vast and sorrowful.

Jade asked,

"What is this?"

Paulo replied,

"*Fado*. The traditional music of Portugal."

Jade asked,

"And *Fado* means…?"

Paulo answered,

"*Fate*."

The impact is so intense that, for a moment,
everything vanishes.

No light. No sound. Not even pain, just a sudden
halt.

The kind of silence that makes time fold in on itself.

And then, awareness.

It takes a few seconds, or perhaps a few years, to
realize where he is.

His mind refuses to return to the previous moment.

Out of fear, and out of incapacity.

It's like trying to grip water. The moment slips
through.

Instead, it moves further back.

To what came before.

To childhood.

To the ancient anxiety of falling.

That primitive lurch of the stomach, the helpless
velocity, the certainty that something trusted has
failed.

But the situation leaves no room for retreat.

Søren must understand what has happened.

He must assess.

He remembers: he wasn't wearing his seatbelt.

But now, there is no belt, no seat, no trace of the

quiet elderly woman who was beside him.

Only he remains, and the sky,

and a ground rising toward him with deadly speed.

His mind begins to calculate.

He recalls the number for gravity: 9.8 meters per

second squared.

Altitude.

Impact velocity.

Like a physics problem he once solved on the

blackboard.

But this time, there will be no grade.

No neat ending.

Death, in its most precise form, is approaching.

Søren believes in science.

He knows how ruthless gravity could be.

He knows nature owed no justice.

And now, in the moment of encounter, he realizes:

This belief offers no comfort.

All it gives him was an obsessive accuracy in

measuring the exact way he will be broken.

How the pieces will scatter.

Truth without consolation.

A fleeting wish passes through his heart:

If only I hadn't let go of the God of Abraham.

If only, instead of *Spinoza's* god,

he had someone who could reach out a hand in this

moment.

Spinoza is elegant in equations.

But in falling silent.

The wind pulls him like a stringless kite.

And then.

He remembers:

He is dreaming.

And in dreams, the soul does not shatter.

Physics is dismissed here.

So, he surrenders.

Let the fall continue.

And a sound emerges,

something between music and absolution,

perhaps Bach.

Yes, it is part of the *St. Matthew Passion.*

And then, he wakes.

With the kind of silence that only comes after

accepting death.

Now, he was awake.

Or he thought he was.

And isn't wakefulness nothing more than the assumption of being awake?

There had been no boundary.

No line. No jolt. No identifiable shift.

Only passage.

Like a breath leaving the chest.

But his heart still pounded.

Fast.

Deep.

Like a rhythm returning from the corridors of death.

As if his body knew something his mind had not caught up with.

From the hallway, the *St. Matthew Passion* was fading out,

its notes dissolving into quiet.

In that moment, something moved in the corridor.

The sound of slow footsteps, a human rhythm in the heavy silence that follows a dream.

Søren rose.

Opened the door.

A woman was walking slowly toward the stairs at the far end of the hall.

He followed.

But the stairs,

those same old winding stairs of the inn,

Spiraled, vague, full of turns that returned you to

where you began.

He lost her.

She disappeared.

And suddenly, he found himself in the lobby.

Silence hung thick.

Like a curtain draped from the walls.

The reception desk was empty.

No one stood behind it.

Even the desk itself felt unreal.

No bell, no guestbook, no open calendar.

Everything seemed staged.

So, he moved toward the main door.

Opened it.

And the cool Lisbon night air brushed his cheek,

with a gentleness that seemed to come from

somewhere far away.

And Søren wondered:

Is this peace… death?

Or a return?

Or just an unnamed moment between the two?

He stepped onto the gravel path.

The pebbles made no sound under his feet.

And just then, he felt the urge to turn back.

To look behind.

To see whether the inn, the Domus Animae, still stood.

He thought:

Maybe if I turned around, there'd be nothing there.

Maybe the building had only existed as long as he wasn't watching it.

Maybe the soul needed absence in order to appear.

And this was only a dream within a dream.

No window.

No light.

No memory of the rooms.

He turned.

And the house was still there.

At least for now.

He sat on a wooden bench by the narrow gravel road.

The air was still cool.

He reached into his pocket.

The pack of cigarettes was still there.

The same one he had bought the day before,

without knowing why.

He took one out.

Lit it gently.

The smoke rose.

Like thoughts not yet shaped.

And in that silence, on that distant horizon,

Søren thought:

Why must I choose how to see him,

when he is everywhere?

He remembered *Alan Watts*:

"You ask me what reality is?

Tell me where you stand.

Reality is not separate from the observer.

It is the relationship itself."

Søren smiled and whispered to himself:

If they ask me about him,

I will say:

Tell me where you stand.

He is in that relation.

Whether he is one thing,

or everything,

or even nothing at all.

They once asked a school of fish:

What is the ocean?

One said,

"I don't see any ocean. I've never seen such a

thing."

Another said,

"Everything except me is the ocean."

And the last said,

"I see nothing but ocean."

The *St. Matthew Passion* was still alive within him.

Like blood moving through his veins.

A story remained untold.

The story of the used book, the one that led Søren to the inn.

He remembered it clearly.

July 5th, more than a decade ago.

He had just begun teaching, his first real academic post. On his commute to the college, he passed a small used bookstore, nestled beside a field, half-hidden, almost part of the farm behind it.

The building looked like it had once been something else, maybe a shed, maybe a stable, now filled with volumes instead of hay. It leaned slightly to one side, as if bowing to the weight of its stories.

From day one, he wanted to stop.

But he didn't.

Used bookstores had always fascinated him.

Why?

Because every book carries two stories:

The one written, and the one lived through it.

The fingerprints of a stranger on a page, the forgotten train ticket used as a bookmark, the slight

warping of a spine from someone's bathroom
steam, they told more than blurbs ever could.
He believed stories stacked like sediment: the
author's voice layered with the reader's emotions,
marginalia, underlines, memories.
A friend once warned him:
"Never lend your books. And if you must, never
mark them.
Your handwriting reveals too much. People can
read your insides through your pencil."
Søren had laughed at the time, but he never forgot
that. It felt strangely true. Some people spoke with
their mouths; others left confessions in graphite.
It wasn't just books.
He felt the same way about scrapyards, abandoned
cars, left behind like shed skins.
The paint faded, seats torn, mirrors cracked, they
whispered of arguments had, music played too loud,
someone crying on the steering wheel.
He dreamed of photographing them. Not because
they were beautiful, but because they were *storied*.
Each one a carrier of context.
Of return.

Of distance.

Of silence.

Equations gave structure.

But stories, they gave *meaning*.

They weren't linear. They curved and spiraled and folded in on themselves, like memory does when it's honest.

The inn, he would later realize, did the same.

Søren had countless bookstore memories, small, quiet revelations that stayed with him long after he'd left the shelves.

They were moments no one else would notice, a whispered title, a dusty sunbeam falling across the name of a forgotten philosopher, the soft bell of the door closing behind him like a curtain dropping on a play.

In his twenties, one of his favorite pastimes was wandering bookstores without buying anything. Back then, there were no chains. No big-box retailers.

Bookshops were *pharmacies for the soul*.

Once, during a late evening commute, he stepped into a small store called *Delight*, in English.

He asked the owner if they had anything on Haikus.

The man paused and replied:

"I don't think so."

Søren raised an eyebrow. "What do you mean?"

The owner looked at him for a long moment.

"I have something better.

Something that's medicine for you."

He returned a few minutes later with a copy of the *Tao Te Ching*, elegantly printed, with Chinese calligraphy and soft black-and-white photographs by *Jane English*.

The verses breathed.

The images exhaled.

And the book lived by his bedside for fifteen years.

He read it in pieces, never in order. When sleep wouldn't come, or when it came too heavily, he'd open a page and let the words guide him back to center.

The cover frayed. The spine bent. But it remained intact, like the soul of a house that has withstood both storm and silence.

But he never stopped at that used bookstore.

Not until his final day as a professor.

On impulse, maybe fate, he pulled off the road.

Nearly got rear-ended.

He heard someone curse behind him.

The road was narrow.

He parked anyway.

Inside, the shop was quiet.

A woman in her sixties stood behind the counter,

silver-gray hair, bright blue eyes.

There was grace in her stillness, and a lingering

beauty that didn't need permission.

She greeted him with a nod.

He tried to vanish between the shelves.

But her voice followed.

"Looking for something in particular?"

He was cornered.

He had a trick for this, a habit perfected over years

of browsing without purpose.

He used to ask for a book no store would have:

"The Collected Works of *John Donne.*"

Once, he'd used the same trick in a shop near

campus.

The woman didn't have Donne, but she offered

Dylan Thomas instead.

He bought it.

As he left, she asked for his number, said she'd call if *Donne* ever came in.

A few days later, she left a voicemail.

"I found it. Five dollars."

He never returned.

And he still regretted that.

This time, he told the truth.

Told the story.

The woman smiled.

"I'm Alice. But not from Wonderland."

He smiled back.

"I'm Søren. I teach nearby."

She added:

"I'm Nordic too, by the way."

He paused.

"Oh, I'm not Danish. My mother was in love with Abraham, the one from the Bible. That's why she named me after a Danish theologian."

Then he added:

"Today's my last day."

She nodded.

"Mine too.

I'm closing the shop. It was never my job. I was a nurse.

After my husband passed, I kept this place going for the love of it.

But now I'm selling the farm.

Moving west.

I've got grandkids I haven't really met yet."

It felt like a coincidence, but not quite.

Something rarer.

Not impossible. Just… improbable.

He asked:

"Do you have anything on old houses? Classic architecture?"

She pointed to the far shelf.

"Architecture section. Back wall."

He found it.

A thick book, full of photographs.

Two dollars.

He paid.

Said goodbye.

And stepped outside.

The light had changed.

Something in him had too.

Was it a calling?

He didn't know.

But he wanted it to be.

Because stories don't just describe the world.

They *summon* it.

He thought of the stories that didn't begin with
decisions,

but with something quieter,

a glance,

a stranger's voice,

The kind of moment that passes before you know
it's changed you.

He is climbing a ladder.

It rises far, farther than it should.

Farther than anything manmade.

No walls.

No roof.

No scaffolding.

Just air, and rungs, and the weight of his own motion.

He doesn't know where it ends.

There is no visible destination.

Only *up*.

He climbs anyway.

The wind increases the higher he goes.

Tugs at him like a reminder.

The rungs grow thinner.

More distant.

His arms tremble, but his mind does not.

He won't fall.

He doesn't look down.

Above him, someone else climbs.

A *woman*, maybe.

He can't see her face, only movement.

Fluid. Determined.

Unhindered.

Her pace is steady.

Her form clean, focused.

He tells himself he is climbing *with* her.

But he knows he is climbing *after*.

Then, the top.

There is no platform.

No ledge.

No floor.

Only a *window*, suspended in air.

A frame of light, carved into the sky.

She reaches it first.

She doesn't stop.

Doesn't hesitate.

Just passes through.

Effortless.

Complete.

Gone.

Søren reaches the window.

He touches the sill.

It is cool and smooth, like stone warmed by memory.

The light spills onto his hands.

Inside: a glimpse.

A desk.

Curtains moving.

A soft glow that seems to know him.

A room he might have lived in.

Might still.

He presses forward.

But the window *resists*.

Not like a locked door.

Not like punishment.

Just… *firm*.

Certain.

Not yet.

He stays there.

Fingertips inside.

Body outside.

Sky all around.

He does not fall.

But he cannot enter.

Not now.

Not yet.

She is climbing.

She doesn't question how high.

The air is thin, but it feels clean.

The wind brushes her arms but never pulls.

She doesn't know where the ladder ends.

Only that she must continue.

There are no walls.

No anchors.

Nothing to fall against.

And yet, she climbs without fear.

The rungs narrow as she ascends.

Her hands never slip.

Below her, someone follows.

She feels him, not as a threat, not as a burden.

As *presence*.

He climbs more slowly.

Carefully.

She does not turn to look.

But she knows it's him.

At the top, the sky opens.

There is no platform.

Only a *window*.

A frame of soft light, suspended in blue.

She reaches it.

Touches the sill.

The air shifts, like recognition.

She doesn't pause.

Doesn't doubt.

She passes through.

Easily.

Completely.

And inside, there is calm.

A desk.

Curtains moving gently.

A quiet she has waited for.

She does not close the window behind her.

She does not need to.

She feels him just beyond the threshold.

Reaching.

And she lets him be.

Søren had long lost his connection to numbers.

He still loved mathematics, its elegance, its inner logic.

The way it once offered clarity in a world too blurred by noise.

But no theorem thrilled him anymore, no axiom or result moved him.

Something had become distant.

A hidden thread that once tied numbers to his life had quietly snapped.

Like a violin string that no longer vibrated, even when plucked.

Not that he ever truly believed in the "real world."

Søren never had faith in something called reality.

In his eyes, everyone lived inside their own version of it.

Realities built out of religion, conspiracy, childhood dreams, trauma, even philosophy or science.

Reality wasn't a singular thing.

It was a collage of meanings, stitched together with memory and belief.

A patchwork of fears and longings, barely held together by language.

And somewhere along the way,

his own meaning-making system.

The framework he had once breathed in.

Had quietly drifted from numbers.

What once was his livelihood, his language, his refuge.

Now felt irrelevant.

As if he had returned to a language he could still speak but no longer feel.

And yet, here he was.

At the inn.

Could this place, this space between sleeping and waking,

between endings and beginnings,

rekindle the fire of that old love?

Could the inn not only connect him back to numbers,

but return their meaning to him?

As a living language,

a way to interpret dreams,

and relationships,

and perhaps even the code of existence?

He wasn't sure what he hoped to find. But he knew what he had lost. And that, somehow, was enough to begin.

And it did happen.

The inn responded to his longing.

Something stirred within him.

And something, maybe the inn itself, stirred in reply.

So, Søren began to notice all the numbers that seemed to belong to the inn.

Room numbers that are added to prime totals. Keys labeled with irrational digits. Clocks that ran five minutes late, always, as if time itself was being nudged into a new alignment.

He began to wonder: was the architecture of the inn itself numerical? Was there a pattern embedded in the floorboards, a code etched into the silence between footsteps?

He remembered that moment.

When he'd called to make the reservation.

A calm voice, like the static of an old radio, had simply said:

"Room 21, Dr. Hossein. We'll see you soon."

No options were given.

No questions asked.

Just a number.

At the time, he thought:

Strange.

Now he understood why.

In the outside world, we assign numbers to people

and places.

License plates, student IDs, phone numbers, and

property codes.

We give the number to the thing.

But perhaps here, in the inn,

people were assigned to numbers.

Or as Søren saw it:

"The room numbers are variables. The guests are

values that fit them."

The inn was a living equation.

After years, the thrill of theorizing returned.

Each guest was placed in a room,

not by preference,

but by correspondence.

Not for comfort,

but for symmetry.

The number came first.

Then the guest.

He felt that room numbers weren't mere labels.

They were coordinates in a higher-dimensional space.

A kind of mapping.

An embedding.

A function.

Each room reflected something:

- Prime numbers for those outside the norm.
- Perfect squares for those trapped in their own order.

The inn wasn't arbitrary.

It was deliberate.

It was alive.

And for the first time in years,

numbers no longer felt sterile or remote.

They breathed.

They meant.

Not just tools for proof and measurement,

but windows into being.

And Søren,

he had been placed.

Not lost,

not forgotten,

but assigned.

Once, while still teaching data analysis,

Søren had opened class with a simple trick.

He wrote a number on the board,

something random, like 55102,

And asked:

"What can you tell me about this number?"

Silence.

The students stared as if he'd spoken a foreign

language, which, in a way, he had.

That number could've been anything,

a ZIP code, a license plate, an ID tag, or none of the

above.

Søren shook his head.

A number, without context, is hollow.

Empty.

Void.

Then he drew a musical note.

Still silence.

Then a letter, J.

Still nothing.

But when he projected an image of an apple, the

class reacted.

Even if you slice an apple, even if you load a truck

with them, it's still an apple.

The meaning remains.

It endures.

It carries.

Then he returned to the notes.

He placed three side by side.

Now there was something to hum.

A melody.

Suddenly, those marks had rhythm, context.

He did the same with letters.

J. Then o. Then y.

Now there was feeling.

Now there was meaning.

Then he said:

Numbers are like that, too.

A single number says almost nothing.

But when they are arranged rightly, they whisper.

They reveal value.

They reveal pattern.

But one question had haunted him:

What gives numbers their meaning?

What draws the line between chaos and form?

And now, in the inn, on a gray sofa in the corner of
the lobby,

Søren found his answer:

Sequences.

He scribbled the early Fibonacci numbers in his notebook:

0, 1, 1, 2, 3, 5, 8, 13, 21, 34, 55, 89, 144, 233, 377, 610, 987…

His own room, Room 21, was in the sequence.

He pulled out his boarding passes from Boston to Toronto and from Toronto to Lisbon:

89 and 144.

Both Fibonacci.

And the page number in that old book where he found the inn?

233.

If he ignored the single-digit entries,

only one number from the remaining sequence

could still be a room number at the inn:

13.

And with that thought, he slowly walked down the gravel path away from the inn,

already composing

the next question in his mind.

It was late afternoon in Paris. Dr. Luc Armand was in his office on Rue Saint-Jacques, the windows cracked opened just enough to let in the sound of passing traffic and a distant bell.

The sun filtered through the old glass in long, diagonal shafts, touching the edges of the bookcases with quiet familiarity. The scent of old paper and Bergamot tea lingered in the air.

On the small table beside him, a yellow notebook lied open, filled with notes in fine, looping handwriting.

The phone on his desk rang, a few minutes past the scheduled session. He lifted the receiver and heard Jade's voice, distant but steady. She was still in Lisbon, delayed by flight disruptions, yet insistent that they speak.

There was something in her tone, not panic, but presence. A gravity that made Luc sit straighter. Jade explained there was something about the inn she could not ignore, something unfinished, something pressing. Her voice carried the weight of intuition sharpened by experience. She didn't want to cancel. She wanted to understand.

Dr. Armand adjusted in his chair, listening intently. The tone of this session would be different, softer, more uncertain, more immediate. But he knew this: they were close. Very close.

He spoke gently into the receiver:

"All right, Jade. I'm here. I can hear you clearly. Let's begin."

"I know it sounds unscientific.

But everything feels like a setup.

First, a mechanical issue with the aircraft, a stupid engine failure.

Then another mechanical issue with the rental car, which diverted me from Paulo's place to this inn.

And when I got here... it felt like something had been dragging me toward it.

As if the inn was waiting for me.

It's a strange place, and yet, I don't feel like a stranger.

Do you remember the dream... the one about the other side of the darkness?

I think I'm finally inside the building now.

And all the emotions connected to the little boy,

they've come flooding back."

Luc's voice was calm and measured, but carrying

an undercurrent of urgency:

"Yes, Jade. I remember.

And what you're describing, this "setup," this

unlikely sequence of disruptions, that's not as

unscientific as you think.

Sometimes the psyche rearranges the outer world to

mirror the inner threshold.

It nudges the path. Alters traffic. Cancels flights.

Not to sabotage, but to summon.

And when you listen, truly listen, you'll notice:

what you call coincidence is often choreography.

You didn't choose this path consciously.

But something in you did choose.

And now, you're no longer circling the architecture

of the dream, you've stepped inside.

You're in the structure.

You're no longer just dreaming about the boy.

You're beginning to dream with him.

This is not a coincidence.

This is proximity.

You are very close, Jade.

Tell me, when you say the emotions returned, what exactly did you feel?"

"I felt his presence, just like in the dreams.

After the dream about the music, the one with the man, I didn't dream for weeks. Nothing.

But last night, I had another one.

We were climbing a ladder, from the earth into the sky. It was surreal, impossible.

There was a window floating in the sky, and I was ahead of him. He was behind me.

And again, I could feel his doubt, not because he didn't believe in the climb,

but because he wasn't sure he could make it.

I reached the window first.

And when I entered the room behind it, there was a sense of absolute peace, complete, almost holy.

I kept the window open, just in case he could make it too.

But he didn't.

And now I think that window… wasn't redemption.

It was a separation.

I have this feeling I'll never see him in my dreams again.

I feel like I've lost something, not like a lost love.
Something else.
And it aches.
It aches like the dream where I left the little boy
alone in the darkness.
But this time, it's not just about care or protection.
It's deeper. It's heavier.
I don't know what it is."
His voice softening, gentler now, the kind of
gentleness that only came with deep witnessing:
"Jade… you didn't abandon him.
You climbed.
You reached the window.
And you waited.
That ache you're feeling, it's the cost of passing
through.
You've moved beyond something.
Not above him.
But beyond the point where the two of you shared
the same place in the dream.
He couldn't come with you, not because you left
him behind,
but because you crossed into a new layer of

yourself, and he, for now, remained in the one below.

The window may feel like a separation…

But what if it's preparation?

You didn't close it.

You left it open.

That matters.

And this ache, this specific ache,

It's not a wound.

It's a threshold.

You're very close, Jade.

To something you've been circling for years.

Do you feel it?

Not in the mind.

In the body.

In the breath.

Do you feel something settling? Or waiting to be named?"

"Close to what, Luc?

The end of the recurring dreams?

The end of seeing a little boy shaking in the cold and darkness?

The end of that ache I feel when I see a child alone in real life, and it haunts me for weeks?

Is it the end of my broken relationship with my
mother?
The end of the chain of heartbreaks, every man I
ever loved pulling away?
I don't know.
I feel lost, Luc.
But I also can't deny this feeling, that something is
about to happen.
Not out there.
Inside me."
Luc's voice was deeper now, resonating like
something ancient but gentle:
"Yes, Jade. That's exactly it.
You're not nearing an end; you're nearing your end.
Not death.
But the dissolution of the version of yourself that
was built from ache.
The dreams, the boy, the ache, the absence…
They were not the story.
They were the scaffolding.
Now something wants to emerge.
Not as a conclusion,
but as a self not wrapped in survival.

The reason you feel something is going to happen inside.

It is because it already has.

The architecture is shifting.

You're not circling your pain anymore.

You're standing in the center of it.

Still breathing.

And what comes next…

There won't be more pain.

It will be the shape you make when you're no longer defined by it.

You're not lost.

You're between definitions.

And that,

is sacred ground."

"It's getting late, Luc, I know you have to catch your train.

If I happen to make it out of this inn, I'm joking, I'll meet you in your office next week.

I don't have any flights scheduled for the next ten days."

Luc, with a warm, unhurried tone, as if time itself had softened:

"Take your time, Jade.

The inn isn't holding you, it's receiving you.

And whenever you're ready to leave,

you won't walk out empty-handed.

Next week, my door is open.

But until then… let the inn speak.

And trust what answers."

One night, the dream changes shape.

It assumes a familiar form.

Søren rushes into an elevator.

The elevator is on floor zero.

His heart is pounding.

Perhaps someone is chasing him, someone unseen.

He presses the button for floor 2.

Waits, breath held.

The doors open.

It's morning.

He steps into a manicured garden.

Everything is precise.

A shallow, clear pool. A gentle fountain.

Silence, except for the sound of water and his own

footsteps.

He walks.

Enters a library.

It isn't large.

But it's complete.

He climbs a stairway.

Stops at a floor marked: 2

No one is here.

But everything is in order.

From a shelf labeled in a blend of Roman and
Arabic numerals, 5-0-8-I-I-III, he searches for a
Persian history book.

He finds it: *Jahān-goshāy* by *Juvayni*.

He opens it to precisely two pages.

Not by accident.

He reads pages 34 and 55.

Takes notes.

Returns the book to its place, according to a small
sign requesting so.

Signs his name.

Writes down his time of entry.

And his time of exit.

Returns through the same garden path.

Takes the elevator once more.

This happens repeatedly.

Not like a cycle.

Not by error.

Like a ritual.

One day, perhaps the fifteenth, perhaps the
hundredth, he pauses by the garden.

Lifts his gaze.

Why do I return home?

Where is home if no one is waiting?

What makes this place different from the one

before?

The questions arrive like echoes.

Like raindrops gliding down a windowpane.

He offers no answer.

There's no need.

And then,

he wakes up.

It is neither night nor day. The sky outside is
grayish gold, as if memory and light have merged.
Søren stands in a long hallway where no hallway
existed yesterday. The walls breathe ever so
slightly. Windows shift locations when he's not
looking. The carpet underfoot grows softer the
longer he stands still.

A distant ticking, not from a clock, but from
somewhere deeper, pulses in time with his breath.
The inn is alive, not with words, but with presence.
Rooms rearrange themselves based on mood. Doors

appear, then vanish.

Portraits once blank now begin to sketch

themselves as he walks past.

Some of the eyes look familiar. Some seem to

follow him. One, he could swear, blinked.

This is *Domus Animae*, the house that is also the

soul, and Søren has finally decided to speak to it.

He doesn't know if he's inside the inn, or if the inn

is inside him.

"I am finally here. And I feel like I never left..."

The Inn replies, voice shifting like wind through

curtains, soft and knowing:

"You never did.

You've walked through cities, languages, loves,

faces,

but your footsteps always echoed in these halls.

You mistook the world for distance.

But this place,

it is not far.

It waits in the exact shape of your return."

Its voice is not sound but sensation, the way warmth

gathers near a fire, or how a forgotten name hovers

just behind the tongue.

"I saw you in my dreams. Sometimes broken, other
times shining like a castle. Old or new, large or
tiny, like a grave.
I saw you at the edge of darkness when I was only a
little boy.
You never invited me in.
I saw you as a collage of my memories. I saw you
as my mirror.
Why are you always changing like a living thing?
Why, even now, do you shift for me,
but appear to others as just a solid, ordinary
building?"
The Inn responds, its voice a blend of shifting
walls, humming floorboards, and the scent of old
books being opened:
"Because you are not the same boy who once saw
me from the edge.
You bring me new eyes each time,
and I shape myself to match what they cannot
name.
To others, I am still, because they are.
They do not listen,
so I do not move.

But you,

you listen with your scars.

You carry silence like a question.

So I answer.

I change because you remember differently each
time.

You call it memory.

But it is creation.

And I,

I am made of what you dare to see."

"Now I'm inside.

I was always looking at my inner self from the
outside.

That's why I used to see a broken soul.

But now I'm inside… and I can see my inner self.

And it's still broken.

Is this the end?"

The Inn replies, its voice low and steady, like rain
beginning deep in the walls:

"No.

This is not the end.

This is the first time you've looked without turning
away.

Broken is not failure.

Broken means touched.

Broken means *entered*.

What you see now, this fractured self,

it is not a ruin.

It is a foundation.

The cracks are invitations.

You are inside now.

You don't need to search.

You need to stay."

"But I never left you.

All your people, if I can even call them people,

know me.

Every single brick remembers me.

I never left you, yet I was still far from you.

My logical mind can't process this.

Do you remember the dream, the one with the

collage of houses?

I went to the basement.

Someone called me to go there,

even though I was certain I was the only one in the

universe.

Was that you?

Were you the one calling me to the darkest rooms

of my soul?"

The Inn responds, its voice shifting from behind

closed doors, between flickering lights, inside the

grain of wood and breath of silence:

"Yes.

That whisper,

that ache disguised as curiosity,

that was me.

I don't speak in sentences.

I speak in nudges.

In the missing stair rails.

In the way a hallway narrows just enough to make

you hesitate.

The basement was never beneath you.

It was inside you.

I call not with sound,

but with absence.

Not with answers,

but with an invitation.

You were never alone in the universe.

You were just alone in your belief.

And yes,

every brick remembers you.

Because you left something on every wall:

your fear,

your longing,

your love,

your will to descend."

"My intuition tells me I should be afraid of you.

But I'm not.

When I arrived here, I felt like I was being

absorbed.

What do you want from me?

If I die… will you be destroyed too?"

The Inn replies, voice slow, like a deep wind

turning pages in an unseen book:

"No.

If you die,

I will not be destroyed.

But I will go silent.

Like an unopened letter.

Like a room that still waits,

with a light left on.

I want nothing *from* you.

I want something *with* you.

You are not fuel.

You are not sacrifice.

You are the only one who can walk these halls with

your name written on the walls.

You built me without a blueprint.

I grew from your questions.

I shifted with your grief.

I opened rooms you weren't ready for, not to

frighten you,

but to show you where light still refuses to give up.

If I absorb you,

it is not to erase you.

It is to hold you.

But I cannot hold what you keep running from.

Will you let me carry what you can't name yet?"

"I won't run anymore.

I've just arrived."

The Inn replies, now as stillness, not voice,

as warmth in the walls,

a door unlocking somewhere behind the silence,

a light turning on in a room not seen before.

"Then rest.

Not as an escape.

But as presence.

The house remembers.

And now,

so do you."

Søren found himself outside the inn, sitting alone
on a wooden bench, a cigarette burning softly
between his fingers.

How had he come here?

He turned to look behind him, the inn stood
perfectly still, as if holding its breath.

Had the enigma been solved?

If he stepped inside again, would it begin changing
once more?

The inn had never been a stranger to him.

But for most of his life, he had been a stranger to
himself.

36 A Conversation in a Hidden Language

The café on campus was busy, filled with the low hum of late-afternoon chatter and the clinking of mugs on wooden tables. The large windows let in the golden hue of a fading sun, and the air smelled of coffee beans and books. Sonya had walked in first, earlier than she said she would. She had taken a seat in the corner, her back to the main counter. She breathed deeply, summoning every bit of the distance she had built in the last few months.
She had no illusions.
The ache was still there, not burning, but persistent. But she was not there to feel. She was there to observe.
Søren's advice echoed in her mind: step outside the narrative, become the narrator.
When Amit entered, he spotted her immediately. He was smartly dressed, casual but calculated, the kind of effort that showed he had thought about impressions, but maybe not about emotions. He walked to her table, uncertain whether to smile.
They both sat. The silence was familiar and heavy.

Sonya had suggested they speak in Hindi, a language both knew well, but one that made the space around them feel private, coded. She had made a quiet joke about nosy students, and he had agreed.

She had learned this from Søren, too.

The English version of her love for Amit was searing, full of emotions, memories, and unspoken grief.

It was a narrative of tears and sighs.

But they had never built a shared story in Hindi.

And that, for Sonya, was the safe distance, the buffer that kept the emotions from spilling over.

She reminded herself:

He was not a villain.

He was a soul.

Lost, maybe. But not cruel.

And now, the observer inside her leaned forward.

Amit:

"Hi, Sonya.

Thanks for agreeing to meet. I wasn't sure you would.

You look... good. I mean, not just good, calm.

Different.

I've been thinking about our last conversation. A lot, actually.

And I wanted to ask you something. But first, how have you been?"

Sonya:

"I'm good.

I've moved on.

I'm focusing on my final year, applying for jobs, that's about it."

Amit:

"That's… that's good. You always had that focus.

I knew you'd land on your feet.

I didn't want to make this uncomfortable.

But I keep replaying a few things I said, or didn't say.

Back then, I thought I was being honest. Clear.

Now I'm not sure if I was just… absent.

Not physically, but emotionally.

I didn't come today to ask for anything, Sonya.

I just didn't want silence to be the last thing between us.

And I know you don't owe me anything.

But if you want to say something, anything, I'll

listen.

I mean it."

Sonya:

"As Sonya with a broken heart, I have so many things I could've said.

But right now, as Sonya watches this from the outside, just observing two souls having a conversation, I don't have anything to say.

It just… happened.

There are so many things in life we don't have answers for.

What happened between us wasn't the end of the world.

It wasn't the end of humanity.

It just happened."

Amit, quiet now, as if something in her calm had disarmed his practiced confidence:

"I don't know why… but hearing you say that made it feel real.

Not better.

Just… real.

You always felt things deeper than I did. Maybe you still do.

I know I didn't show up the way you needed. Not

even close.

And I know you didn't want explanations or
apologies.

But thank you for not turning it into bitterness.

That's rare.

If there's anything I can do, not to fix anything,

just… as a person who once meant something, you

can tell me. Or not.

I'll understand."

Sonya:

"You can do one thing for me,

don't feel guilty.

Don't try to compensate.

And please, don't offer sympathy.

Maybe what happened was supposed to happen.

Yes, you hurt me. Deeply.

But I've tried not to see it from a moral perspective.

Even from that angle, you didn't break any promise.

You just walked away.

And I chose to see it not as betrayal, but as

something existential.

You were trapped in your narrative.

So was I.

That's why, eventually, I could process it more easily."

Amit, looking down, his voice slower, quieter, a little less guarded:

"I had never heard anything like that before.

And maybe that said more about the kind of people I'd been around than it did about you.

You were right, I was trapped. Still am, maybe.

And I didn't even see the walls.

But you did.

And you stepped outside.

Not just from us… but from yourself.

You aren't bitter, Sonya.

You are free.

And I don't know if that makes me feel sad… or grateful.

Maybe both."

Sonya:

"You were never supposed to do anything for me.

Not even an apology.

The story between you and me never had many words.

It was more a conversation of bodies than a dialogue of souls.

And if there was ever a conversation of souls,

it was rare.

Very rare.

Do you remember my mother?

You saw her.

I decided not to become like her.

Not to live *inside* the pain.

Not to let it shape my identity.

I didn't want pain to define me.

I chose to *observe* it.

Not live *within* it,

but *with* it.

Because there's no escape from pain.

But there is a difference.

When you stand *with* your pain,

it no longer defines you,

you define *it*.

And then your soul is not trapped by sorrow.

It expands.

It grows large enough

to hold pain within it

without being swallowed.

I gave meaning to the pain I carried.

And for that,

I thank you,

for helping me realize

that *I have a soul*."

The inn was alive.

And it wasn't just a building with rooms, occupied
or vacant.

It was a river, a living, continuous being.

The rooms were like droplets:

distinct, but never separate.

They could drift, vanish, or merge,

but all were part of the same current.

On the third evening, Søren wandered into the
forest behind the inn.

He passed the mist's edge, down a narrow path lost
under moss and leaves.

And in the hush, he came upon a hidden clearing.

A quiet stream crept between the stones.

Its surface was dark and still.

Søren sat there a long while.

Not waiting for anything.

But something arrived.

"How does one connect with the soul of existence?

Not metaphorically, truly."

He had long believed the world wasn't a dead
machine.

It was a living whole,

a system with breath and will.

With a soul.

He believed the universe had an inner life.

Had spirit.

If this were true, the question was not:

"Does the world speak to us?"

But rather:

"Can we hear it?"

Søren imagined a telephone,

one of those old models with twisted cords.

Heavy. Nostalgic.

From another century.

This phone wasn't connected to anything,

except something higher, meant for a singular

message:

A calling. A mission. A meaning to life.

He played a game in his mind:

"If this phone were your only way to receive the

message of your life,

would you know how to use it?"

He saw three possibilities,

three different ways humans relate to life, to

destiny, to meaning:

The first path: waiting for a call from beyond.

In this scenario, the phone may ring at any moment,

and that's beyond your control.

You must keep the line open.

Stay close.

Listen.

This is the path of faithful waiting,

the way of prophets, of pilgrims, of those who

believe in sacred timing.

Moses on *Mount Sinai*.

Muhammad in the cave of *Hira*.

Mary in the moment of *annunciation*.

They didn't seek God,

God found them,

because they were ready. Listening.

Søren called this sacred timing *the sacred moment
of the butterfly*.

He learned it from *Nikos Kazantzakis*,

who, in *Report to Greco*, told of a butterfly

struggling out of its cocoon.

Impatient, *Kazantzakis* blew on it to help.

But his warmth rushed the process,

and the butterfly emerged with crumpled,

incomplete wings,

and soon died in his palm.

He called it the greatest burden on his conscience,

and learned:

Don't rush.

Don't force.

Trust the rhythm of life.

The second path: searching for the number of the

universe.

In this case, the phone in in working condition,

but you don't have the number.

Still, you believe such a number exists.

So you begin the search.

This isn't waiting,

it's longing in motion.

This is the seeker's way.

The mystics, the poets, the lovers,

wandering in scorching plains,

fasting in silence,

writing to a beloved who may never read their

words.

They didn't dial a specific number.

They looked for signs.

Not just to be certain,

but to be faithful to the possibility.

They believed:

"Knock, and the door shall be shown.

Knock again.

And perhaps it will open."

In this view, the seeker doesn't make the call,

they listen more deeply than others.

Search the libraries,

the stars,

forgotten shrines,

their own breath,

for anything that might echo that number.

This reminded Søren of *Rumi,*

of *Hallaj,*

of *Francesco of Assisi,*

and of *Saint Mirabai,*

those rare ones

who did not escape suffering,

but sang from within it.

The third path: the connection is already open.

There is no number to dial.

No call to wait for.

The line is live, like a hotline.

You just must pick up.

This is the path of unity, of non-duality, *Advaita*.

Breath and source are not separate.

They have always been one.

The only barrier is forgetting.

Søren thought of *Ibn Arabi*.

Of *Adi Shankara*. Of *Meister Eckhart*.

He is not elsewhere.

He is here.

Within.

Always has been.

"I was never hidden from you; so why do you seek me?

I was closer to you than your own jugular vein."

Each path speaks a truth:

Some wait.

Some search.

Some remember.

Søren didn't know which he was.

Maybe all three.

Maybe none.

But the message was one:

You are connected.

Not someday.

Not if you become worthy.

Not if you're lucky.

Now.

You only have to notice.

The stream whispered among the stones:

Connection is not rare.

What's rare is *attention*.

Most don't pick up the phone.

Some never even hear it ring.

Others fear what they might hear.

Søren stayed still and let silence do its work.

Then rose, turned toward the path to the inn, and

began to walk.

The inn was waiting.

It always was.

38 THE MOMENT BEFORE THE MOMENT

Where the Distance Between Sleep and
Wakefulness Is Just a Breath.

[Jade]

Jade woke to the soft *ding* of a text message.

It was from her Polish co-pilot:

"Captain Galani, our aircraft is grounded. We need

to catch the next flight back to Paris."

Without a word, Jade silenced her phone.

The window was open.

A light breeze was gently swaying the curtain.

From the hallway, the sound of a violin drifted in.

Jade wasn't well-versed in classical music,

but if she had asked someone,

this would have been Schubert, *Serenade*.

She wrapped a square jade-colored shawl around

her shoulders.

Curious, and a little uncertain,

she opened the door

and stepped outside.

[Søren]

Søren was already awake.

Sitting on the edge of the bed, he turned on the

lamp.

The window was open.

His dream had ended, not abruptly, not lost.

Almost all the numbers had arrived,

except for two:

13 and 377.

In the dream, the woman hadn't appeared.

No familiar or unfamiliar face.

No house either.

But there had been form.

Stillness.

And a calm drawn from silence.

He didn't know if it was his heart

or his ears

that caught the sound of the piano

rising from the hallway.

One of his favorite pieces:

Chopin's *Spring Waltz*.

He pulled on his brown coat

and stepped into the corridor.

Something was calling him.

The staircase no longer misled him.

The mansion had softened, tamed.

The rooms no longer bore numbers.

The numbers had done their part.

[Jade]

The hallway was quieter than before. Morning light slid in like breath through the windows, brushing the edges of the old wood floor.

She didn't know where she was going. The inn had no logic. It never had. But something, some *pulse* in the house, was guiding her.

She passed a staircase and paused.

It curled upward, familiar in a way that felt cellular.

Not remembered, *recognized*.

[Søren]

He traced his fingers along the railing, the spiral beneath his hand warm like it had been touched a thousand times. He had dreamt of this staircase. But the numbers were gone.

No Fibonacci markers.

No patterns.

Just silence.

And then.

That scent.

Sandalwood.

Cedar.

It came not from the air, but from *time*. From memory that didn't belong to this world.

[Jade]

And then she heard it.

A voice. His voice.

Not speaking to her, but *speaking the phrase*, like always:

"It is all about numbers."

She stopped moving.

Her skin tightened. The hallway vanished. The inn, the floor, the day, *gone*.

Only the voice remained.

[Søren]

Søren turned slowly.

A woman stood at the end of the hallway.

He did not know her.

He had never seen that face.

And then,

that scent.

Sandalwood and cedar.

Something inside him leaned forward,

quietly certain:

It's her.

The woman from Room 13.

He didn't know how he knew.

He just did.

[Jade]

She stepped forward. Closer.

Her heart did not race,

it settled.

Like a boat reaching shore

after a long, unforgiving storm.

Softly, she whispered:

"You used to say this in all the dreams.

All these years.

It was always you."

[Søren]

Søren blinked.

Her voice touched something deep within him.

He asked:

"You... heard me?

You always smelled of sandalwood and cedar, too."

[Jade]

Jade nodded gently.

And for the first time in her life,

she was utterly still.

Planted.

Answered.

Seen.

A soul looked back at her.

And remembered the dream beyond the dark.

This time, she had no doubt.

He would step into the darkness,

but she would anchor her gaze to him,

so he would never disappear.

[Søren]

Søren felt a bird singing in his blood.

He no longer needed numbers.

13 and 21,

not just a pattern,

but meaning.

Not a sequence of the lifeless.

But a thread of soul.

At last,

someone had taken his hand

and brought him home,

into the house,

into himself.

He remembered the dream beyond the dark.

This time, he would not hesitate.

He would walk into the darkness,

because he knew,

her gaze was a thread

that would never let him vanish.

[Both]

And for a moment, neither moved.

The house, like them, held its breath.

The End

AFTERWORD

This was the second attempt.

The first one, over 200 pages,

died on the operating table.

Why?

Because it was only *my* story.

And a good story isn't just about the self.

It's about connection,

about finding a thread that ties your silence to

someone else's.

That's why Jade came along.

This story lived in me for more than a decade.

It began with a used bookstore by the side of a road.

That part is true.

The bookstore was real.

So was the pull I felt every time I passed it.

I never bought a book there.

I should have.

But the feeling stayed,

like a seed buried too deep to sprout.

Over the years, the stories grew.

They didn't come in order.

They didn't even come as stories.

Just fragments.

Dreams, all true dreams.

Moments that wouldn't let go.

They stayed with me.

Tangled in thought.

I couldn't write them.

But I couldn't abandon them either.

I needed something to bind them.

A thread.

A frame.

A reason.

It didn't come right away.

It came much later,

quietly, unexpectedly,

when the final scene appeared in my mind.

That's when everything began to make sense.

The inn.

The numbers.

The dreams.

Some stories are not told in words.

They are told in waiting.

In living with the questions.

In returning again and again to the same haunting

silence.

To seeing yourself

reflected

in the mirror of devastating questions.

To weeping,

but choosing not to complain.

No story is truly beautiful

unless its ending is a release.

Like an equation whose elegance

lies not in its proof,

but in the stillness of its solution.

S. H.

- Gann, Ernest K. *Fate Is the Hunter: A Pilot's Memoir*. Paperback ed., Simon & Schuster, 1986.

- Jung, Carl G. *Answer to Job*. Translated by R. F. C. Hull, Princeton University Press, 1952.

- Weil, Simone. *Gravity and Grace*. Translated by Emma Craufurd, Routledge and Kegan Paul, 1952.

- Bodhi, Bhikkhu, translator. *The Connected Discourses of the Buddha: A Translation of the Samyutta Nikaya*. Wisdom Publications, 2000.

- Schopenhauer, Arthur. *Parerga and Paralipomena: Short Philosophical Essays*. Translated by E. F. J. Payne, Clarendon Press, 1974.

- Spinoza, Benedict de. *Ethics*. Translated by Edwin Curley, Penguin Classics, 1996.

- Heidegger, Martin. *Being and Time*. Translated by John Macquarrie and Edward Robinson, Harper & Row, 1962.

- Jung, Carl G., editor. *Man and His Symbols*. Dell Publishing, 1964.

- Buber, Martin. *I and Thou*. Translated by Walter Kaufmann, Charles Scribner's Sons, 1970.

- Nietzsche, Friedrich. *Twilight of the Idols*. Translated by R. J. Hollingdale, Penguin Books, 1990.

- Jung, Carl Gustav. "The Transcendent Function." *The Structure and Dynamics of the Psyche*, translated by R. F. C. Hull, Princeton University Press, 1960, pp. 67–91.

- Von Franz, Marie-Louise. *Number and Time: Reflections Leading Toward a Unification of Psychology and Physics*. Translated by Andrea Dykes, Northwestern University Press, 1974.

- Jung, Carl Gustav. *The Archetypes and the Collective Unconscious*. Translated by R. F. C. Hull, Princeton University Press, 1969.

- Berkeley, George. *A Treatise Concerning the Principles of Human Knowledge*. 1710.

Edited by Kenneth P. Winkler, Hackett Publishing Company, 1982.

- Kierkegaard, Søren. *Fear and Trembling.* Translated by Alastair Hannay, Penguin Classics, 1985.

- Ekman, Paul. *Emotions Revealed: Recognizing Faces and Feelings to Improve Communication and Emotional Life.* Times Books, 2003.

- Johnson, Vida T., and Graham Petrie. *The Films of Andrei Tarkovsky: A Visual Fugue.* Indiana University Press, 1994.

- Jung, C. G. *C.G. Jung: Letters, Volume 2, 1951–1961.* Edited by Gerhard Adler, translated by R. F. C. Hull, Princeton University Press, 1975.

- Whorf, Benjamin Lee. *Language, Thought, and Reality: Selected Writings of Benjamin Lee Whorf.* Edited by John B. Carroll, MIT Press, 1956.

- Lucy, John A. *Language Diversity and Thought: A Reformulation of the Linguistic Relativity Hypothesis.* Cambridge University Press, 1992.

- Tagore, Rabindranath. *Gitanjali: Song Offerings*. Translated by the author, Macmillan, 1913.
- Kazantzakis, Nikos. *Report to Greco*. Translated by P. A. Bien, Faber & Faber, 1965.